GRUB

Spineless Wonders
ABN98156041888
PO Box 220 STRAWBERRY HILLS
New South Wales, Australia, 2012
www.shortaustralianstories.com.au

First published by Spineless Wonders 2019

Typeset in Adobe Garamond Pro

National Library of Australia
Grub / Tanya Vavilova
1st ed.
ISBN 978-1-925052-79-4
A823.4

A catalogue record for this
book is available from the
National Library of Australia

This project has been assisted by the Copyright Agency Cultural Fund.

COPYRIGHTAGENCY
CULTURAL FUND

GRUB

TANYA VAVILOVA

Contents

Grub

When we get to the restaurant, we're bustled inside, given a corner table and plastic menus with grease-dappled pictures. It's the sort of place where plastic grapes hang from the ceiling and faded posters advertise some long-ago dance troupe. I like it a lot.

What do you want to get, babe?

Mon always gets the same thing here, and I'm happy to eat whatever she orders. It's always been this way.

A side of Asian greens?

Sure.

Braised eggplant?

Sounds good.

It's all the same, really. You like something, or you don't like something – the stakes aren't exactly high.

The plates and bamboo steamers arrive one or two at a time, steam rising like hot breath in winter. The waiters are brisk, silent. I add a little soy sauce and chilli to the bowl, pass Mon the chopsticks.

The red sun outside looks like a bauble. I watch it sink.

How was work? Mon is asking.

Sammy burnt fifty finger buns.

How?

She was at front of house, making coffees, and forgot about them. Thank god the first batch turned out fine so we had enough for the after-school rush.

Imagine all those angry kids.

Smashing up the glass cabinet with their tennis racquets.

I used to love them. *(Mon gets wistful about everything.)* That sticky pink icing with flakes of coconut.

Heaven. Actually, I ate one today.

Where's mine?

Thought you were still on your sugar-free diet.

Yeah.

So?

Right.

Mon is always on one kind of diet or another, just like her mother. Last month she was basically fasting, and we didn't go out for dinner once.

The chatter of the other diners fills the poky space. I catch the eye of a passing waiter. Could we please have some more green tea? I ask. He nods, picks up the teapot, returns with a fresh one, the steam curling from the snout.

You want a top-up? I ask Mon, before refilling our tiny cups.

The dumplings are lovely and translucent. Little sweating parcels of tofu and spinach, eggplant, egg and chives. We've fallen into that knee-deep silence that comes from hunger. I don't mind. I'm biting into my second dumpling, when—

I spot a white squiggly thing.

Christ, I whisper.

What?

There's a grub in this one.

What?

I extend the dumpling towards her, skewered by a chopstick.

Mon winces. Oh, *gross*.

Yeah.

The white head of the little grub pokes its head out of the filling.

Is it moving?

Is it?

We take a closer look.

Nah, definitely dead.

Caterpillar or maggot? I ask. *(I think we both know what it is.)*

If we were eating pork and cabbage dumplings, it might be a caterpillar. In egg and chive, definitely a maggot.

I put the dumpling on the side of my plate.

Mon stares at it. We should say something, she says.

Why? We want to come back here, don't we?

I don't want to come back here, she says.

What, over one little grub? We've been coming here for years. It's practically our second home.

I pick up another dumpling, inspect it, take a cautious bite.

I can't believe you're still eating them, she says.

I'm checking for grubs as I go along.

She crinkles her nose.

Oh, come on, I say. It's just a grub.

You're a grub. And *it's* a maggot.

Are you going to eat those?

She shakes her head.

Have the braised eggplant then, I suggest, pushing the plate towards her.

Mon is still sulking when we walk up Jones Street to our basement flat.

Oh, hon, you're not still upset about the dumpling, are you?

I just wanted us to have a nice night for once.

We did, didn't we? *(It's best not to indulge Mon's melodramatic tendencies.)*

Do you have the keys?

Yep, I say, pulling the keychain from my pocket.

The padlock's a little stiff; you have to jiggle it a few times.

After you, m'lady, I say.

Mon hops in the shower while I get straight into my t-shirt and into bed. Somewhere behind the headboard, the water pipes whistle and scream. They sound angry, broken, old. The whole house is falling apart. The whole block, too. On the walls, here, the paint's peeling like skin off a dancer's heel.

Mon's calling from the hall.

What? I can't hear you.

I stare at the whirling rotors of the ceiling fan. We got it installed last summer. Sounds like a helicopter taking off. Not exactly peaceful.

Mon's in the doorway, hair wrapped in a lavender towel.

The bathroom hooks fell down again, she says. I've draped our towels over the chairs.

I'll have a look tomorrow.

Is everything in this place held together with double-sided sticky tape?

Practically everything, I say.

You're not having a shower?

Nope.

She flops down beside me. I can't believe you ate the dumplings, she says.

Are we still talking about this?

What if you have worms now?

Why would I have worms?

You ate a worm, didn't you?

No, I didn't. *(I put the offending dumpling to the side.)*

Mon's always been fastidious, clean. Lining up our shoes neatly by the door, wiping away blue smears of toothpaste from the sink. Washing her hands until they're red-raw. I've had to be the counter-balancing influence in our lives.

When she finally stops talking and falls asleep, I watch the rise and fall of her chest. I imagine what it would be like to make a clean break, to start afresh. I know I would never do it. We're too entwined, been through too much together.

Mon emerges in her undies, her little belly curving over the elastic.

Brekkie? she asks.

I'm on it. Toast and eggs?

Sounds great.

I carve the stale bread into slices.

Did you wash your hands? she asks.

'Course I did. (*I didn't.*)

You're not trying to strengthen my immune system again, are you? All you're doing is spreading germs around by not washing your hands.

Yeah, yeah.

Okay, what can I do to help?

I give her the cherry tomatoes to halve. Watch her wield the serrated knife like a surgeon. She's always had a certain precision about her, a sharpness.

We eat brekkie on the couch, feet up on the coffee table. Mon wants to call someone to take a look at the black mould in the bathroom.

I don't think it's black mould, I tell her.

It's mould and it's black, isn't it?

But just because the mould is black doesn't mean it's the dangerous type of black mould.

I'm calling someone anyway.

O-kay. *(I know when to surrender.)*

The eggs are a little rubbery, but that's the way I make them now, for Mon. She's always worrying about salmonella.

While we're talking, I catch Mon glancing at my hands.

What are you doing?

Nothing. I'm not doing anything, she says.

You're being weird.

No, I'm not.

Worried about me not washing my hands again? I ask.

Can you cut me another slice?

I do what I can with the hunk of bread. You really need an electric knife for it.

We continue eating and reading the paper. I comment about something interesting on page four, but Mon shushes me – she's reading a different article on page five. About the end of the world, she says.

While she's getting changed for work, I find a stray bread crust under her chair and eat it. I feel rebellious, and only a little bit grossed out.

After work we carry a bottle of wine and glasses up the fire stairs and out onto the roof. From here, you can see several blocks to the west, the smokestacks of the sardine factory rising in the middle distance. The pollution, all those particles in the air, softens the pinks and purples of the setting sky. Makes it gorgeous, a sunset from our parents' time.

We like to celebrate the end of the working week. I pour the wine out while Mon drags some crates over from the corner. I watch her peach butt wiggle as she bends down. She kicks the crates towards me.

Cheers, love, I say, raising my glass. Thank fuck it's Friday.

Thank fuck it's Friday.

You know, this city is goddamn beautiful from up here. All those red bricks among the high-rises, and the arch of the bridge. You ever climbed it?

The bridge?

Yeah.

Nah. I don't know if you're allowed to anymore. Someone died last year, didn't they? Some tourist from Sweden.

Tourists, huh.

Yeah.

Mon pulls out a surgical mask from her pocket.

What the hell are you doing? I ask.

Protecting myself, she says. Sitting up here is like smoking a pack of cigarettes.

Who says?

The news.

How are you gonna drink your wine?

She whips out a plastic straw, pleased.

I laugh. *(She's full of inconsistencies.)* Okay. Suit yourself.

Her concern about pollution doesn't make sense in this grubby, overpopulated basin. The whole city's basically a giant petri dish.

Hon, do you think you're taking things too far?

She doesn't answer.

I watch her eyes above the mask scan the skyline. They land on a DANGER. ASBESTOS REMOVAL IN PROGRESS sign across the street. They've been removing the toxic stuff for years, she says.

You want a top-up? I ask, lightly.

She nods, and we clink glasses, but something has shifted between us.

Later that night, coming out of the toilet, I notice Mon eyeing me.

What, hon?

I didn't hear the taps run.

Are you kidding me?

Did you wash your hands?

Of course I did. *(I didn't.)*

Don't lie to me.

I go back into the bathroom and run the taps while inspecting my ears for wax.

You don't want to spread MRSA, do you? she asks when I join her in the kitchen.

Mon, please, enough with the superbugs. It's too much.

It's important to me that you wash your hands, she says.

Well, it's important to me that you don't nag.

I won't nag you if you wash your hands.

Mon saw a psychologist a few years back and now adopts the language of Resolving Conflict in Five Easy Steps. It's very annoying.

I'm gonna have a beer, I announce, opening the fridge.

And E. coli, she says. You could spread E. coli by not washing your hands.

The pop of the bottle top dulls my anger nicely. I'm no longer listening to Mon.

When she comes home from work on Monday, I lean in to kiss her. She gives me her cheek.

What's wrong? *(I'm genuinely perplexed.)*

Can you brush your teeth first?

Christ, Mon. Why?

You've been eating sausage rolls at the bakery, I can tell.

So?

It makes me feel anxious when you neglect personal hygiene. *(I want to scream at her.)*

I refuse to brush my teeth.

We eat tomato soup in silence, each of us on our laptops. I look over Mon's shoulder – she's watching a muted video of simulated tsunamis.

Daily, Mon asks me to wash my hands, brush my teeth, disinfect my body. This goes on and on and on and on and on and on and on and on and on and on and on and on.

One day the following week, I come home to find her wearing a bright yellow Hazmat suit.

Hey, hon, I say. That's a cool outfit.

Yeah, I got it at the community centre.

(Our local community centre is always preparing for the apocalypse.)

I got one for you too, she says. *(Christ.)*

She reaches under the table. Here, put it on, she says. Let's do a practice run.

Maybe later, I say, looking at the suit.

I'd really prefer it if you wore it now.

I don't have the energy to argue. Worked ten hours at the bakery today, cutting cookies into cute Christmas shapes for the holiday season. So we cook spaghetti in full hazard suits. It's cumbersome, constrictive. After struggling on tiptoes in the Hazmat suit to reach the bowls on a high shelf, I give up and serve the pasta up in mugs.

Here, I say, handing one to Mon.

We sit down at our dining table – actually, pallets arranged in a Jenga stack.

Um, why are we wearing these suits again?

Mon ignores me, continues to scoop up the spag.

Umami-rich, she says.

She's talking about MSG. Apparently, tomatoes naturally release monosodium glutamate as they're cooking. That's why you can eat so much of them, and you don't get full, she says.

Hey, love, I'm burning up in this suit...

The pasta is spicy and it's thirty degrees in this concrete box. My skin is stuck to the teflon.

It's coming off, I tell her.

Suit yourself.

I laugh, but she doesn't register her own pun. Unzipping and unpeeling, I emerge like a caterpillar from her cocoon: glistening, alive. I drip sweat into my mug of pasta.

Mon doesn't look too pleased, and we finish eating in silence.

I drop a hunk of cheddar onto the floor, and it catches strands of hair, dust. I eat it anyway. Later, I find myself licking the outside of the fridge, just to see what it tastes like.

Mon is spending more and more time at the community centre preparing for the apocalypse. Wearing black t-shirts with slogans like WARMING WARNING, THE BURNING ISSUE, and THERE IS NO PLANET B.

They have an underground bunker, Mon says. And cans of baked beans and big plastic tubs of croutons. I've been to the Earth Welfare Centre – a pastel pink weatherboard by the railway line – and can't imagine it withstanding more than some light rain.

I imagine the lot of them, sitting on plastic chairs, drinking kombucha, talking nonstop about superbugs and rising sea levels. Mon's rising panic.

I keep turning up to my shifts at the bakery and bringing home bags of leftover bread. Mon's rarely home these days. I eat all the finger buns myself.

On Thursday, we invite my friends from the bakery over for dinner. When Mon opens the door, Alex and Bonnie startle, and I realise they're shocked by her Hazmat suit.

Immediately they ask what's wrong.

It's a precaution, Mon says, against disease agents.

I butt in – Mon's a little worried about germs, that's all.

Alex looks scared.

Before you come in, Mon says, there's just one small thing I like to do.

She corrals my guests into the back alley, asks them to strip off their clothes.

What the hell?

It's okay, I whisper. It's best to humour her.

Mon aims the fire hose, and Bonnie screams. Their bodies bend double under the jet's spray. Alex is bracing herself against the fence, her feet in a puddle. Their bodies glisten under the water and the sun.

I watch the rust-coloured water run down the drain.

When it's all over, I chuck them some beach towels.

Let's get dinner on, Mon says, coiling the fire hose.

We sit at the Jenga-table, Bonnie's blond hair dripping onto the cement floor. Mon passes around the hand sanitiser, saying, Better safe than sorry, don't you think? We each squirt some clear jelly onto our palms.

I'm about to plate the stuffed peppers when Mon snatches the plates away to spray them with disinfectant.

The peppers, when we eat them, have a slight chemical taste.

Sorry about all this, I say, when Mon disappears to wash her hands for the fifth or sixth time.

I watch my friends exchange glances.

On Friday I stay up late, waiting for Mon to come home. It's 10 pm, then 11, then midnight. I think about cutting the Hazmat suits into pastrami strips with scissors.

When she turns her key in the lock, I'm ready.

She's surprised to see me sitting on the couch.

Where have you been? I ask.

I told you, doing drills at the centre.

I can't do this anymore, I tell her.

She sits down opposite me on the over-stuffed sofa.

I'm trying to prepare, she says. Prepare us for the difficult times ahead.

It's too big, for me, I tell her. Too big to tackle.

Like climate change, she says.

I'm sorry, I say, feeling helpless.

She watches me pack my things into a suitcase on wheels. I chuck the leftover finger buns on top of my clothes, and, out on the kerb, hail the first bus I see.

I check into a motel with a neon Vacancy sign. Eat the finger buns with dirty hands while the trains chug past outside. Stay in bed for a week until the bakery calls, wondering where the hell I am. I start turning up to work again.

A few months later, a new baker starts with us. Soon we're living together. Our domestic routine feels familiar. While Alla cooks, I wash the plates. Don't like to leave them piling up. When she eats week-old ricotta and gets sick, I'm the one to call the nurses' hotline. I double-wash apples and peaches, no longer eat food off the floor.

I hear through the grapevine that Mon has met someone from the Earth Welfare Centre, that they're happily preparing for the apocalypse together. Saw her on telly once, too, protesting outside the sardine factory. She was wearing her cute SAVE THE REEF tee, and her words rang sharp and strong and true.

For our one-year anniversary, I take Alla to my favourite dumpling place. The waiter recognises me, nods.

We sit at a corner table under a plastic vine of purple grapes. Alla is looking at me.

Yes, love?

She stretches her dumpling towards me.

I panic. What is it?

Look at the glossy spinach, she says, so lush. Like a fucking rainforest.

I laugh with relief, call the waiter over. Could we please get another serve of these ones? I ask.

Dirt

The earth was red and dry, burnt. A couple of ghost gums straggled across the rock, among the grasses and dust. A dead roo lay by the side of the road, its ears cocked to the side. No-one about.

Someone or something had dug a big hole in the earth, so deep you couldn't see the bottom. Anne and Jay stood at the rim, careful not to slip in, and assessed its depth. Their tent was only a few metres away, but they hadn't noticed the hole in the night.

When Anne had gone to brush her teeth this morning, she'd almost fallen in.

I think there's something down there, she called to her girlfriend.

Jay knelt on the bare earth, and peered in, her back scorched by the sun.

Can't see nothing.

To the left, see? Near that groove. A coin? Look!

Maybe.

Do you reckon it's a wishing well or something?

In the middle of this shithole? Don't think so.

Anne rummaged in her pockets for some coins. You got some change? she asked.

I got two bucks, but I ain't losing it down that hole.

She loved Jay, but *Christ*. It was forty degrees, maybe more, and she was stinking hot, could feel the sweat pool in her too-big bra, the one she'd nicked from Jay.

Anne?

What?

C'mon, we better get going. Don't wanna be pitching our tent in the dark again.

Anne pouted.

Oh babe, Jay said, and with a flourish tossed a cold coin into the hole.

They listened for the sound of it land.

While Jay tore down the tent, Anne sat in the dirt and rolled up their K-mart sleeping bags. Tight like jam rolls. Her gran had loved to make jam rolls. Even though her hands shook, she'd baked one for Anne's sweet sixteen. A week later, she took her last breath. A slice of jam roll left in the fridge.

That was almost ten years ago now. The grief still came and went.

Anne fastened the ties around their sleeping bags. They had matching ones, of course. She put them to the side, and started on the bedrolls.

How quickly she'd adjusted to being on the road. To having grubby hands and dirty feet. And meals that came out of cans. To sunburn and ant bites. She no longer squealed when something bit her at night.

Shame to be leaving so soon, but they had to be in Camooweal in six days. Even though she was tired, she didn't complain. Jay wouldn't have stood for that.

Their campsite had spread out from the myall tree. Tarp and towels. Books and clothes and cups and plates. Anne piled the leftovers in the esky and used her weight to close the lid. One last sweep. There – empty Heinz can in the scrub. Last night's dinner. She bent to pick it up.

The sky was blue-blue. No clouds to soften the sun's glow. The outlines of the rocks and trees sharp like blades.

Anne sat on a stump and watched Jay pack the tent poles in their pouches. Methodical, that's what Jay was. Had a map in her mind of what she needed before she started a job.

Need a hand? she asked.

Nah, why don't you start packing the van.

Anne wiped the sweat off her face with the hem of her dress. Yeah, okay.

They didn't need to talk much anymore. The comfort of being close was enough.

It was hard to cram everything into the van. Jay was a real planner – they'd packed spare tyres, toolbox, tarpaulin, first-aid kit, water to last them a week.

Anne squashed the sleeping bags and bedrolls between a birdcage and record player in the back. Jay loved junk sales. Picked up all sorts of broken, battered things.

She wedged the tarp under the back seat, chucking the stripy pillows on top. Jay helped her lift the esky in.

Anne stretched her nimble limbs. Hon?

Yeah.

Who do you think made it?

The upper half of her girlfriend's body had disappeared back inside the boot. Her sunburn sang. It'd start peeling in a day or two.

Hon?

Yeah.

The hole. How'd it get there?

Jay emerged holding a crinkled map. She knelt and spread it out on the dirt, using rocks to pin the corners down.

That thing's been folded and refolded a million times.

Jay said nothing, but followed the squiggly lines with her finger.

Aren't you curious?

Curiosity killed the cat.

You sound like my gran. Also that's such a stupid cliché.

Jay laughed, throaty like a galah. I forgot you went to uni-ver-sity, she said, pulling Anne towards her.

Chapped lips and body heat.

Anne pulled back. You taste like Bushells tea.

Better than breakfast.

They'd had baked beans, again.

C'mon then, Jay said, taking Anne's hand. She led Anne down the track past the scrawny gums, their boots kicking up the dust.

The hot wind pushed the air out of Anne's lungs. None of this dry, oven heat back home. She missed the slap of salt, the sea breeze.

Been months since she was in Mackay. The last time was when she introduced Jay to her strange little family.

Her girlfriend had been calm and cool. Like she'd always been in that weatherboard house among the lemon myrtle and grevillea.

Gem and their dad John took a shine to her straight-away. When Anne said Jay liked old electronics, her dad grinned and pointed the way to the shed. Just wait till you see what I have in there.

Anne and Gem smiled at each other.

You really like her, huh.

More than that. Anne looked at her shoes.

Gem whooped and hugged her sister.

It was a first for Anne. Love hadn't come into it before.

While they caught up on each other's lives, they set the table with the nice plates and cutlery. Like their gran used to. Anne picked some daisies from the garden and Gem filled an empty jam jar with water from the tap.

When they called lunch, Jay emerged with an armful of dusty, precious junk: an old radio and turntable, a rotary phone, some silver boxes and tangled leads.

John was beaming. And you girls said there was nothing good in there.

They had crayfish and salad and a crusty loaf that Gem had baked. A jug of water with floating lemon-wheels. Everyone said the food was great.

A brush turkey bobbed across the lawn, then another. She'd missed seeing them. A flock of galahs flew overhead. Iced VoVos, they used to call them, like the bikkies.

Jay told stories about her life in Adelaide. How she'd worked in bike shops and pubs, moved around a lot. John shared some anecdotes about Anne, even though he wasn't around much back then. She let him.

He told them about how she'd laid out her crystals on the verandah under the full moon. To harness the celestial energy. We all believe in some odd things, don't we?

Why don't you go for a swim? he said. Show Jay our local paradise. You know how to swim, Jay?

In a pool, sure.

They'd laughed at that.

Anne taught Jay about currents and stingers. They splashed in the still blue until their eyes stung with salt.

Jay took off her bright orange bottoms under the water and rinsed out the sand, before putting them back on.

They swam a little way out, away from the families and kids, and kissed beneath the sun's burning eye. Jay cupped Anne's freckly face as if to tell her something.

*

There it is, Anne said.

The hole looked smaller somehow.

It looks like someone filled it in a bit, she said.

What, since, like a couple of hours ago?

Yeah.

Looks the same to me.

Anne knelt by the edge and looked down.

Careful, babe.

Anne craned her neck forward. There's definitely something down there. Look! Her body was taut like elastic.

Oh, babe.

I really think there's something down there.

Jay squatted on her haunches and squinted into the hole. I don't see anything, she said.

There's something down there.

What, aliens?

Don't be stupid, Anne said. It's bones. Look at that glint. A grave, or something!

Jay stood up. Come on, babe, let's go.

No, look!

Anne perched like a swimmer on a diving block. Her head down, body angled for the leap.

Please. Stop. You'll fall in.

Anne said nothing. Jay took her arm and tried to pull her to standing, but Anne twisted away and lost her footing.

The inside of the hole was damp and cool. Nice. Like lying on tiles.

She touched her left ankle. It hurt, but not *that* much. Probably a sprain.

…Anne, are you okay?

If she stretched her arms out, she could touch both sides of the hollow. She felt the grit under her nails – must've tried to get a purchase on the way down.

Jay's coin was down here, somewhere. And the bones, where were the bones?

Anne?

When her eyes adjusted, she saw the outline of Jay's head peering over the lip of the earth. She looked pretty, the sun bouncing off her shaved head.

Babe, are you okay?

Yeah, Anne managed. Sorry, I can't … I think I busted my ankle.

Can you move it?

Yeah, a bit.

Okay. That's good. Sit tight. I'm going to get something from the van.

I ain't going nowhere.

As a kid, she loved hiding under their house on stilts, among the spiders and trash. She'd take her lunch down there. A ham sandwich in a brown paper bag.

You wanna be eaten by rats, her gran said.

I'm no scaredy-cat.

Don't ya come cryin' to me when the rats start nibblin' ya toes.

She leant her head back against the cool earth and closed her eyes.

Jay was gone for a long time. Maybe she wasn't coming back. Who really knew where they stood, anyway? The others had slammed screen doors, roused the neighbours. That wasn't Jay's way. She'd get in the van and drive away quietly. Leave Anne standing on the porch.

Anne dug around in the dirt. The hole didn't seem so mysterious now that she was in it.

She untied her Blundstones and eased her purpling foot out. Kicked the boot out of the way and stretched her leg. Pain, low and deep, like a drum.

When they'd first met, Jay was wearing Blunnies and denim cut-offs. She'd picked a seat at the bar and ordered a beer and pulled out a paperback.

Anne hadn't seen anyone come in with a book before. What are you reading?

Postcards from Surfers.
Oh! I love Helen Garner.

After her shift, she sat down with Jay and called for two more beers. Sharon the manager winked at her, and said, On the house. She believed in romance.

Maybe now Jay was sick of her. She wouldn't be the first.

At least it was nice and cool down here.

She felt woozy. Like after an anaesthetic.

Anne?

Oh, she was still in the hole. How funny.

Anne?

Yeah.

Had to go through the whole bloody car but I found the old rope.

Thought you weren't coming back.

You goose.

Anne smiled and stretched her arms over her head. She felt her pockets. Watched the rope slither down like a snake and, pitching forward, caught it in her hands.

Got it, she called.

She tied the rope around her torso, once, twice. Like they'd taught her at Girl Scouts. Tucked the Blunnies under her arm.

Okay.

She heard the car door slam, the engine start.

Here we go.

The rope went taut in her hands. It pulled her up to standing, and she let out a yelp. Banged an elbow against a jagged rock.

Feet dangling.

As she climbed higher, the smell of dead roo hit her. She was going to be sick.

One last pull and her head crested the earth.

Jay cut the engine, and Anne slumped forward onto the red dirt.

*

In the ocean that day, Jay had held Anne's face in her hands, and looked at her funny. I'm falling in love with you, she said, sighing.

You make that sound like a bad thing. Anne laughed. Like a disease or something. Jay, I've loved you for yonks.

They swam and splashed until the sun set and their lips turned purple.

They were lying on the lumpy mattress in the back of the van, Anne's manky foot propped up on a cushion. And Anne high on codeine.

Jay?

Yeah.

Got something for you.

What's that?

Anne smiled and placed the dirty gold coin in Jay's palm.

Oh, babe. Jay laughed, leant over to kiss her.

From their position on the pillows, they could see the hole. Wasn't anything magical anymore, just a hole that one of them had fallen into.

They watched the sky turn a dusty pink. The colour of pale roses.

Saint Vladimir

Girl, you want to catch a cold?

I look at him blankly.

Get off that porch.

It's okay, I tell him.

Sergei is stuck in the old country. He has a terrific fear of cold surfaces, ice cubes and wet hair.

Sergei, I say, we have enough to worry about here, what with leptospirosis-carrying rats. Remember poor Charlie in Redfern?

He walks away at that, leaving me on the porch with the groceries. I unwrap a Chupa Chup and suck on it thoughtfully. I've been hoarding lollies for years.

Charlie died of kidney failure after a giant rat cornered him in the kitchen and bit a hunk out of his ankle. It's all the neighbours talked about until a Day-Glo spider straddled Kim's baby. But that's another story.

I'm still thinking of Sergei when I get up, my knees creaking like rusty hinges, and make my way home.

The bare trees loom above me, making arches against the chrome sky.

I pass the children's hospital on the corner: a white, rectangular building with prams parked out the front. A kid wails from the top floor.

A woman in a beanie leans against the wall and eyes me suspiciously. Her child is probably dying of dysentery.

I walk past.

Dandelions grow on the sidewalk, grey and fluffy, seeds ready to fly off and germinate, ever hopeful.

The street is almost empty, except for some young hoods on skateboards. They spy my raggedy coat and let me be.

Everyone is just trying to make a buck.

Without Ari, I don't know what would've happened to me. No, that's not true; I do know. I would've ended up in a baby factory. It's a way for the desperate to be housed, fed and clothed.

I turn the corner and here we are: home.

My habitation could not really be called a *flat*. I mean, it wouldn't appear on RealEstate.com or anything.

I live in the basement of an abandoned Russian Orthodox Church. St Vladimir's: the dude who brought Christianity to the Kievan Rus' and later minted coins and imported wine. So yeah, my people like him a lot.

I pull open the tiny timber door, and prop myself on the ledge, then push myself, feet first, into the cramped space.

The dust motes rise about my boots.

Ari will be back soon and I want to make sure dinner's ready. We are a post-gender couple, but, you know what? I'm the better cook. One time, Ari served up death caps on toast. It was appalling.

After a few false starts, I get the wood stove going.

The vegie sausages are bobbing in the little pot. The label on the can says *Classic Vegetarian Sausages in Gravy*, though what's classic about it still eludes me. We found these in the kitchen of an abandoned boarding house.

At least the stove is hot, the flame licking the sides of the copper pot.

It hasn't risen above ten degrees in weeks. This basement is dank and overgrown. Vines creep through cracks in the plaster, making green barbed-wire nests in corners.

Under the glow of the oil lamp, you can just make out the creepy crawlies between the pots and pans.

I hear Ari climb through the window as I'm ladling the sausages.

Perfect timing, Ari says, by way of greeting. Vegetarian sausages, again?

What d'you expect? Shepherd's pie and a nice garden salad?

Ari sighs.

It's hard to keep upbeat when the world's ending.

We hunch over the steaming bowls in silence.

I'm chewing on a carrot or potato – it's hard to tell because every vegetable in the can is round and brown.

All of a sudden I drop my knife.

Ari watches me. Points to the knife. Alright, what's that mean?

I sigh. It means, I say, we'll have a visitor, a male visitor.

You don't really believe that, do you?

There are soup flecks on Ari's face. I don't say anything, because what's the point? Neither of us have jobs to go to anymore, or anyone to impress. We smell like pubescent boys after Little Athletics.

You want some more? I ask, before turning away to do the washing up.

Afterwards, we climb the stairs, go through the trap-door and emerge at the back of the old church.

The light is hazy, heavenly. Almost silver.

I think about commenting on this but can't formulate the right words.

There are fewer pews now than when we first moved in.

We use about a pew a week for firewood.

I came here when we were growing up. With my parents and brothers. I imagine I can still smell the incense from the priest's golden thurible, curls of sweet-smelling smoke.

The iconostasis has been stripped bare. After the last economic downturn, the icons were pilfered and sold on eBay for a fraction of their real worth. Some of them dated from the sixteenth century.

Is it time for another pew? Ari asks me.

Yeah.

I breathe all the air out of my lungs.

You still feeling bad about it?

Yeah, I admit. Stupid, huh?

Why don't we grab a small pew today?

We push the old oak bench out the door, and carry it around to the basement window.

Where's the axe?

Behind the crapper, Ari answers.

Do you have to call it the crapper?

Oh, that's right, I forgot we were referring to the pit by the fence as the powder room. My apologies.

I can't help but smile.

We take turns smashing the old oak, our breath hot and misty in the night.

Later, I'm standing in the basement, and Ari passes the lumber to me through the window, telling me to be careful.

Of course I'm careful, I say.

We chose this place initially because it has a functioning fireplace. Rare these days. I think fondly of the years of electric heaters and reverse-cycle air-con: the dry heat, the ease, everything pre-programmed and predictable.

We know we are lucky to have a roof and four walls.

I watch as Ari gets the newspaper and twigs smoking.

Ari smiles at me. Where are the sleeping bags, pet?

I drag our deflated nylon caterpillars to the fireplace, get as close as possible to the heat.

The orange flames are rising and licking the ancient oak.

It feels sacrificial, burning those pews. Not that I'm religious or anything, not for a long time.

Ari curls their body around mine. We are two spoons in a Hello Kitty sleeping bag. I'm too tired to be embarrassed by how far we've sunk.

The fire, the fire, the fire.

I love you, pet, Ari whispers, as I drift off to a troubled sleep.

When I wake, Ari is gone. We like to say, *to work*. What they really do, I have no idea. I respect their need for secrets.

Meow Meow is stretched along the window ledge. She likes to catch the morning sun, warm her tiger stripes.

Hello, I say. Hello, little cat.

She waves her pink paw pads at me.

I'm distracted, worried about running out of church pews. If only we'd squatted in a Catholic or Protestant church: those folks had a pew for everyone.

I watch Meow Meow arc across the floor, land on my sleeping bag, her pink nose twitching at the air.

Hello, I say, again.

She rubs her flank against me, and we meow at each other.

She just arrived one day. Wet and mangy, just like us, and Ari had said, well why not?

She's our fur baby now. The accusation slung at millennials fulfilled: selfish, childless, homeless, jobless, penniless. Dog and cat crazy.

She turns a green eye towards me.

What's wrong? I say. You're cold, huh?

She wriggles under my woollen jumper and settles somewhere above my navel. A living hot water bottle with fleas.

I throw more lumber onto the fire, and stay in bed reading *Cancer Ward*, as Meow Meow kneads my stomach.

She purrs gently and at some point I nod off.

In the early evening, Ari returns triumphant. They've pilfered some hospital blankets for us – you know, those white waffle ones – and some instant coffee. If you're not squeamish, there's stuff to be found in old nursing homes and hospitals.

Where'd you get those? I ask.

You want coffee or not?

I nod, gratefully.

We read our books and drink Moccona, ensconced in our own private worlds. Mine is the aftermath of Stalin's great purge.

Meow Meow splits her time equally between us, jumping from my lap to Ari's then back to mine.

When the sun sets, Ari gets up and turns on the torches and solar-powered lights.

The globes blink on and off: a lonely school disco.

Eventually, I pull myself up to brush my teeth.

Sloshing the rainwater around my mouth, I think of gingivitis before spitting out the window. Someone moves in the dark.

My heart thumps.

Who's out there? I hiss.

Silence.

Sergei, is that you?

Yeah, he says.

What are you doing out there?

I saw smoke coming out your chimney. I'm cold, Shell.

Since government officials took over the terraces, it's been even harder to find a good squat.

Alright, you idiot, I say. Come in then.

Sergei clambers through the window, thick legs first, and lands sprawled on all fours. Meow Meow slinks forward and sniffs him suspiciously.

It's alright, cat, I whisper.

Sergei is complaining of the cold when Ari saunters in from the powder room in the nude.

Arghhh, says Sergei.

Who's this then? Ari asks, looking at me.

This is Sergei. From the old country.

I'd spoken about him before.

Welcome, Ari says, to the basement of Vladimir's Russian Orthodox Church. A late twentieth-century marvel, all weatherboard and mould.

Sergei is staring at Ari's crotch.

This is a sacrilege, he says.

Church or crotch? Ari says, noticing the special attention.

Sergei appeals to me.

You want somewhere warm to stay or not? I ask.

He turns his back to us and mumbles something to Jesus. We watch from a respectful distance.

Okay, I will stay, Sergei announces.

Fine.

I set him up on a pile of cardboard boxes by the fire, and give him a hospital blanket to keep warm. He prays quietly in the dark.

When he drops off to sleep, Ari gets into my sleeping bag, and we curl our limbs around each other, like animals in a David Attenborough doco.

I am dreaming about my father's collection of icons when I hear a scream.

Sergei is standing above us with a pickaxe.

What the hell are you doing? Ari yells. Put that goddamn axe down.

Sergei? I say.

He lowers the axe and stares at it – as though unsure how it got there.

I look at him closely.

I think he's sleepwalking, I say.

Sergei, why don't you put the nice axe down? There you go, easy does it. Right down, on the floor. That's it.

Ari takes the axe gently away, while I coax Sergei back into bed.

There you go, gently does it.

Let's tie his ankles, Ari suggests.

Sweet dreams, Sergei, I whisper, as I tighten the ropes.

Christ almighty, Ari says, climbing in beside me. He could have killed us.

Yeah. I shrug. Something will eventually get us.

(I'm thinking of the rats or the police.)

Even still, Ari says, we should probably keep him tied up at night.

So we do.

We try to get rid of him. At first we suggest we need some privacy, you know, as a couple: he doesn't seem to understand. Then I tell him my father is visiting: Sergei says he'd be very pleased to meet him. We suggest it's getting a little crowded with the three of us, to which Sergei says, But we're almost blood. We're not, I tell him firmly. But still, he won't leave. He threatens to put a hex on us if we try to force him out.

With each passing day, Sergei's religious mania reaches new heights. Today, a week after he first moves in, he decides to re-create a Russian Orthodox service.

Come on, he says, wearing a black robe dredged from god knows where.

Ari and I follow him up the stairs and through the trapdoor, holding hands.

His cassock brushes the dusty steps.

Ari looks afraid.

When we reach the top, I see he has pushed the iconostasis to the side and is standing in the sanctuary, hands raised to the crumbling ceiling.

He is singing in some Slavic liturgical language, howling and stamping his boots on the faded carpet. I suddenly feel very afraid.

Is this for real? Ari asks.

I think we should humour him, I say, sitting down on a pew.

Stand up, he commands. Are you infirm?

Christ.

I jump up, flushed.

We stand silently, listening to Sergei sing in a deep baritone.

Pacing the sanctuary, he swings a smoking eucalypt branch side to side in a parody of a once-familiar ritual, a conflation of multiple traditions.

Come, time for the wine, he announces.

We bow our heads and wait our turn.

I don't want to drink from his cup, Ari whispers.

Remember the axe? I say.

What is this stuff? Ari asks.

The blood of Christ, Sergei says solemnly.

On our way out, Sergei tears us a strip of lavosh bread.

Isn't it supposed to be leavened bread? I ask.

You want to bake some?

He makes a good point. We bow in thanks.

After you, he says, and follows us down the stairs.

When Sergei goes out one morning, Ari announces, Enough is enough.

He's got to go. I agree.

Meow Meow lollops over and sits on my feet. I get the sense she doesn't much like Sergei either. He's too erratic for her, singing liturgies one minute, screaming and murderous the next.

We decide to give him another week.

And then we will kill him.

It's regrettable, really, but ethics are for those at the top of Maslow's hierarchy.

The only thing that stumps us is method.

We pace around the dusty basement, from the hallway sink to the fireplace, back and forth, thinking but also keeping warm.

Arsenic? Ari suggests.

Too nineteenth-century Britain.

Gun?

Too Chicago. Not to mention messy.

Well, why don't you suggest something, Shell?

I propose botulism. People die of it all the time. From eating jams and pickles bought at market stalls decades ago.

No-one would suspect a thing. Not that the police would trouble with the likes of us, but Sergei's relatives might, if they come looking.

I know a woman, Ari says.

Who?

She specialises in the deadly bacterium, is all Ari will say.

On the fateful day, I cook dinner, laying out three plates, the one with the chipped edge for Sergei. His green beans came from a poorly sealed jar.

Thank you, he says, as I pass it to him.

I almost feel bad then.

Ari looks at me sternly. You have to be all in, they said earlier.

I watch Sergei chew, forcing food into my mouth so as not to alarm him.

We are sitting on upturned milk crates around a milk crate coffee table. You make do with what you have. When glitter was banned for environmental reasons in 2025, people threw the stuff out. I'd decorated the crates with glitter-glue love hearts and stars.

Where's our next source of wood coming from? Sergei asks.

Stanmore. There are a few stumpy trees left there, Ari says.

How far?

Not too far, we'll carry it piece by piece while one of us stands guard.

Those rough sleepers are hungry and mean. Millennials, mostly. Global disaster smooths out class differences though, at least after a certain point, so lots of rich folks are out scavenging, too.

I continue shoving forkfuls of nettles into my mouth while Ari tries to keep the conversation light.

Sergei volunteers to do the dishes.

Oh, thank you, I say, alarmed.

He's never once done the dishes since he moved in.

I cast a glance at Ari who shrugs.

I feel really guilty now.

I move my milk crate closer to Ari and whisper, Did we just make a terrible mistake?

Ari tells me to shut it.

I close my eyes and listen to the clang of dishes.

Sergei is singing a Cossack lullaby, elbows deep in water.

And then in the middle of the night, it starts.

Sergei is screaming.

I race over to his cardboard bed and, kneeling down, untie his ankles.

You okay? I ask, knowing full well he's dying.

Ugh, he says.

Ari shines the torch in his face.

His eyelids are droopy, facial muscles slack.

Ugh, he says again.

Ari catches my eye.

Fresh air, they suggest.

I know they just don't want a mess in here.

We support Sergei under the arms, and help him out the basement window. He vomits right over the ledge.

We push his bum up and over, and climb out after him.

He slumps down against the weatherboard wall, and I squeeze his floppy hand.

He vomits again.

The sky is purple velvet. The only sounds are the long-haul trucks chugging along Cleveland.

Meow Meow settles on my lap.

It'll be over soon, Ari says, gently. They are never normally gentle.

Sergei swings his head wildly from Ari to me, but I can tell his vision's shot. Blurred, doubled.

You'll go to heaven, I tell him, squeezing his hand. And get to drink all the kvass you want.

He vomits at that.

And then he slumps forward and convulses.

By morning, he's dead.

Fuck, Ari says.

Fuck, I say back.

Sergei was only the third person I ever killed. It really got to me.

We wrap his body in a blue tarp, and carry him through the gate to the backyard.

Ari disappears, leaving me with the corpse.

I keep watch, though against what, I don't know.

When they come back, they're holding a pickaxe and two beanies.

Here, they say, handing me one, it's minus five out.

If we're honest, I can't see the point. So what if my ears freeze off?

We take turns digging a Sergei-shaped hole in the clay. It's hard going.

The fig tree hadn't borne fruit in years, not since I was a kid, but we thought it'd be a nice gesture. I'd like to be buried under a tree, wouldn't you?

We swing his body into the hole on the count of three.

Ari doesn't falter once.

The service is sombre.

We pour the goon in a cup and take swigs from it. I burn a eucalypt twig and Ari says a Hail Mary. We thank Saint Vladimir for the wine and the horses, and for converting to Christianity.

We each sprinkle a handful of dirt on Sergei's body. Then we stick a wild purple flower on top. The cat pees on the heap.

I like to think we covered all our bases, Ari says.

I reckon we did.

Are you crying?

I dunno. Maybe, I say, ducking away.

At first we are joyous. We sleep like babies. Burn pews. We celebrate with leftover goon. We dance. We wake with hangovers. I make cream of broccoli soup. Even Meow Meow seems happier.

But then, just as suddenly, the dark shadows come alive at night. The light bulbs flicker on and off. Pink and purple Day-Glo spiders come out of their hidey-holes. A cold gust sweeps through the basement.

We try to stick it out, but we can't sleep, can't eat, can't shit.

We can't stay here, I say, there's too much bad juju.

Ari shakes their head, says, We should've just moved in the first place, pet.

Soon after, we abandon the improvised religion, and pack up our things. Meow Meow follows us out the basement window, bouncing alongside us down Cleveland Street.

Where we headed? I ask Ari.

I know a place, they say.

Like you knew a woman?

Ari puts an arm around me. Shoosh, they say, gently.

Meow Meow jumps onto my shoulder.

Up ahead, at the intersection, there's an old studio with the words Urban Yoga. White against black, decidedly modern. The windows are blasted, but apart from that, it looks okay. It's still standing.

I know immediately that this is the place.

Shall we go up? I ask.

We hold hands and take the narrow steps up to our new temporary home. Our newest religion. Meow Meow leading the way.

Artichoke Hearts

Felix gets off at her usual stop, taps off and takes the stairs two at a time. The sky is the same indigo as her jeans, clouds looking ready to burst.

She crosses the road where the IGA logo glows red and white. The building looks freshly painted, the glass doors Windexed to a perfect sheen.

A woman exits the bottle shop clutching a brown paper bag. Her gaze lingers on Felix. And then she collects herself and strides down the street, a man in a cap following her at a distance of two feet.

Felix takes this all in, before walking through the sliding glass doors of the supermarket.

She heads straight for the canned and pickled goods – the marinated peppers, the jars of olives, artichokes in oil – except they're gone. Moved someplace else. She picks up a packet of spaghetti from the shelf, puts it down.

It takes three loops to locate the canned goods in aisle six.

As Felix presents the jar of artichokes to the cashier, the woman smiles at her, but doesn't say anything.

'Thank you,' Felix says.

The woman says nothing.

Snatching the jar, Felix strides out the glass doors.

It's about to rain. The sky crackles like bacon on a pan. Felix has been a vegetarian for twelve years.

Across the road, the park is small and grim. Felix walks past the empty swings, past the monkey bars, choosing a bench under the fig tree. This is what happens, she thinks, when you tell a customer to *lump it:* you end up on a park bench in the middle of the day.

No-one else is about. Even the birds have gone away.

She unscrews the lid of the jar. Her artichokes come all the way from Italy. Marinated in oil with parsley, chilli, garlic, lemon. She's never been overseas; it doesn't matter.

She dips her fingers in the marinade, plucks one artichoke, chews it carefully. The oil drips down her chin. The hearts are slippery, difficult to pinch and pincer. She plucks another then another and another.

The woman from the bottle shop crosses the road without looking. Her red coat and Doc Martens belong in this city. Her brown paper bag is gone. The man in the cap, too.

The woman cuts across the park, negotiates the bulging tree roots. She pushes her fringe out of her eyes.

The first drops of rain are lazy, languorous.

Felix looks up at the clouds.

And then the woman in the red coat is standing beside her.

'Can I sit here?' she asks.

'If you want.'

Felix considers the jar of artichokes, then the woman's slender fingers, microbes, disease. 'Would you like an artichoke?' she asks.

'Um, sure.'

The stranger dips her fingers in the oil and comes up with an olive.

Felix is surprised, but says, 'I guess they're processed in the same factory.'

'Are they?'

They pass the jar back and forth. Once or twice their hands brush. Felix feels a tiny jolt each time, ignores it. Neither says a word.

A raindrop catches on the woman's eyelash, refracts the light.

As the rain gets heavier, Felix pushes her hood over her head, but neither woman moves.

'What happened to the bottle?'

'Huh?'

'I saw you come out of the bottle shop. You bought some wine?'

The woman shakes her head. 'That wasn't me.'

'And the man – what happened to the man?'

'I don't know what you're talking about.'

The woman hugs herself to keep warm.

It rains harder, the drops beating against the tin rubbish bin. If Felix closes her eyes, she could be back home in Geraldton. Instead, she's here, in this shallow, mean city. Jobless, friendless, restless.

The rain puddles in their laps.

'You should have the last one,' the woman says.

'You sure?'

'Have it,' the woman insists, a hand on Felix's knee. 'It's yours.'

The last heart is sweet and juicy.

And then the woman in the red coat is gathering up her things. 'Thanks for the artichokes,' she says. 'I better be going, but maybe see you tomorrow.'

Felix considers those words. She holds the empty jar and watches the woman disappear into the trees. She thinks of running a hot shower. Turning the heater on. Wrapping herself in blankets. She tucks the jar in her satchel and stands up.

On her way home, she passes the fruit shop and the pub with the go-go dancers. A woman in a yellow raincoat pushes open the door, looks at the sky.

When Felix reaches her block of flats, she sees someone has left the entrance door open.

She takes two flights up, patting her pockets for the keys. The stubborn door opens with a groan, lets out a gust of stale air.

Felix strips off her wet clothes, and turns the rusty taps in the shower. Wishes she owned a bath.

Her jeans sprawl on the tiles like another pair of legs.

She adds her empty artichoke jar to the stash under the sink. They look nice there, like old friends. The saved marinade is the real treat – for a special occasion.

Felix stands under the showerhead and watches the tiny room fill up with steam.

The next day, Felix wakes refreshed. Wonders if she's made a new friend.

It's another chilly, drizzly day. Coat and scarf weather. Gloves and beanie.

She buys another jar of artichokes from the smiling but silent cashier. Hopes for a magic olive, like a four-leaf clover. For luck, good fortune.

When she arrives at the park, the woman in the red coat is already there.

'Hey,' the woman says, patting the bench.

'Hey. I'm Felix, by the way.'

'Hannah.'

Felix sits down, puts the jar of artichokes between them. The park is theirs again. No-one else is about.

'Artichoke?'

'Thanks,' Hannah says, reaching for the jar. 'I bought some chips. You eat chips?'

They have a feast.

A grey butcherbird watches them from the fig tree.

Felix wonders if the woman is jobless, but it doesn't seem right to ask. And then she notices the manicured nails: turquoise.

The only sound is the light rain and the crunch of chips. They are crinkle-cut, chicken. Felix vaguely wonders if she should be eating them – are they vegetarian? – but it doesn't matter, not really, because she has a friend.

When she looks up, Hannah is studying her profile.

'You have a nice nose,' she says.

Felix is shy.

'I wish I had a nice nose like yours.'

Hannah squeezes her knee.

'What I wouldn't give for a nose like that.'

They watch the butcherbird impale a lizard on a stick.

'That's nature for you,' Felix says, before plucking another artichoke.

'Shame there's no olive today.'

'Yeah, I was hoping—'

A man zig-zags across the park.

It's the man in the cap.

Felix's insides spin like a washing machine.

'Hannah,' the man booms, 'are you coming home?' He opens a broad, black umbrella, holds it out.

'Yeah,' she says, then to Felix, quietly: 'Another time.'

Felix hopes she means the same time tomorrow. 'See you,' she calls, but they are already gone.

The butcherbird looks down from its branch.

The next day Felix waits in the park, but Hannah doesn't show up.

The day after, Felix stays in bed reading comics.

On Thursday, the stars align, and Hannah and Felix sit under the dome of the slippery dip. The rain batters the moulded red and yellow plastic.

'I missed you the other day,' Hannah says.

'Same here.'

Their legs are touching in the cramped space. Pink bubble gum is stuck to the sole of Hannah's Doc Marten.

They pass the jar of artichokes back and forth.

'They come from Italy,' one of them says.

'Like tomatoes and pasta.'

Hannah touches Felix's face. 'You've got a little fleck of artichoke there,' she says, gently brushing it off.

Felix turns pink.

Hannah's nails are gold today, like the artichokes.

'There you go, all gone.'

The artichokes are salty, acidic. Texture like paper. They could be eating raffia.

'Two ninety-nine a jar,' Felix says.

'Bargain.'

Two myna birds play on the swings, like kids.

'I like your red coat.'

Hannah grins. 'Ta. It's a Lisa Ho original, from Vinnies.'

Felix touches the fabric, catches her reflection in the round, metallic buttons.

'It's gorgeous,' she says.

Hannah's lips are lilac, chapped. She smiles.

The wind changes direction, the rain coming sideways.

Water slaps their cheeks.

'Another artichoke?'

'Thanks.'

They keep eating.

Eventually, Hannah says, 'Dave will be wondering where I am.'

And then she slides feet-first through the blue tunnel, waves and is gone.

They meet up the following day, too. Felix brings artichokes, Hannah a bottle of Sprite. They talk a little, laugh. The fizzy drink makes them burp. And they make a plan.

On the seventh day, Felix drags a shopping buggy to the park. It rattles like a gift.

Hannah waves her over to the fig tree. They share red wine in a silver bladder.

Later, they bump along the road with the buggy. And then they're standing in front of a peeling door.

Felix follows her friend up the stairs.

Their gumboots quack on the lino.

'Dave's out,' Hannah says.

She jiggles the deadbolt. 'So this is me,' she says, gesturing to the combined kitchen-dining-living.

'It's nice.'

'Yeah, it's alright.'

Both women are shivering from the cold and wet. They'd sat in the park for hours, until some kids with sticks came along.

Hannah thinks for a moment, says, 'Should I run us a bath then?'

Felix looks at her shoes. 'Go on, then.'

'There are some towels in that wardrobe.' Hannah points behind her.

The wardrobe is mint green, double doors.

'It's lovely,' Felix says.

'It's IKEA.'

As Hannah's getting the bath ready, Felix wanders in with the towels. 'Wish I had a bath.'

'This afternoon, you do.' Hannah glances behind her. 'You want to get the buggy?'

Felix wheels it from the front room, down the tiny passage between kitchen and bathroom. She takes the empty jars out lovingly one by one, and lines them up around the bathtub.

'So why *do* you save the marinade from the artichokes?' Hannah asks.

'I just always have.'

The room starts to fill up with steam.

Felix has been waiting for this moment a long, long time.

The two women kneel in front of the tub and unscrew one jar at a time, pouring the marinade in. Flecks of garlic, chilli, green float in the steaming water.

A petal of artichoke escapes from a jar.

They strip their clothes off, and Hannah tests the water with a toe. 'Nice and hot,' she declares, before stepping over the lip.

Felix hugs her chest, slipping in opposite.

'You're shy, huh?' Hannah says. She is taller than Felix and her apricot-breasts sit above the watermark.

Hannah lights a coconut candle, resting it on the edge of the tub. The flame dances and spits. The room smells like a spa and a pickling factory.

'Is marinade flammable?' Hannah says.

'I dunno.'

They laugh at that. How funny if their skin caught fire, then the room caught fire then the flat then the block then the street.

Hannah throws her head back and washes it in the marinade. Her forearms are covered in tiny scars.

'Come here,' she says. 'Let me wash your hair.'

Felix turns clumsily around in the bath. Her back to Hannah, she looks out the window that faces the grey street.

The rain spits at the leaded glass.

As Hannah massages her scalp, Felix feels herself loosen, sink further into the water. Both women smell of vinegar.

Afterwards, Felix half-leans out of the tub, picks something off the floor.

'Shall we crack one open?' she asks, holding up a fresh jar.

'Definitely.'

They chew the artichokes, saying little. Felix rinses her arm in the water. And then their knees bump in the tub, and they giggle. A little water spills over the lip.

Hannah drops a rubber duck in the water, and they watch it navigate the sludge. Felix remembers being bathed with her baby sister, the two of them squealing and splashing, driving their mother wild.

Hannah tops up the hot water. They eat some more artichokes.

Felix works up the courage to ask about Dave.

'He's my soulmate,' Hannah says.

The yellow duck nods in agreement.

Felix remembers the first day they met. 'Why did you lie about coming out of the bottle shop with Dave?' she asks.

'I didn't want him to get in the way—' she cups the water in her hands, letting it cascade '—of all of this.'

Felix does not ask any more questions.

They chew quietly, passing the jar between them. And then Hannah dips her hand in the jar, and

'—an olive!'

'You found the four-leaf clover!'

They hold it up to the flickering globe, marvel at this message from the gods. This

green olive in a jar of artichokes.

'We should split it,' Hannah says. 'I know. Come here,' she says, pulling Felix towards

her. 'Let's bite into it at the same time so the good luck can't escape, you know?'

Felix doesn't know. 'Okay,' she says, bravely.

Hannah positions the olive in Felix's mouth then leans forward, bites down on her half, their lips and noses touching.

Felix blushes, tingles.

A diamond beetle flies in through the window. Blue-black magic.

At this signal, Hannah nods, and the women tear the olive in half with their teeth.

They are giddy with luck.

The beetle crawls along the soggy bathmat.

Felix wishes she had a whole jar of olives so they could do that again and again and again. She's never had a friend like Hannah.

When the sky turns red and orange, they decide to get out of the tub but it's hard to find their footing on the slippery porcelain. They sink back into the artichoke juice, shrieking, laughing, then they try to stand again, grab on to each other's arms, sink back, stand, sink, stand, sink, laugh, giggle and grope, until the water cools, and Felix pulls the plug.

Whipped Cream

When we get to the aquarium, the first thing I notice is the cock-and-balls graffiti on the glass. And then the hairline cracks, red buckets on the floor collecting drips. A bunch of tired-looking femmes ogle the last two sharks in the tank, with fins moving half-heartedly, the water a murky green; they seem sad at the turn their lives have taken.

Georgia gives me a little push towards the oldest looking woman in the group.

'Go on,' she mutters. 'She's yours.'

I paste a grin on my face and saunter over to the tank.

'Hi!' I say, brightly.

She turns around, smiles. 'Hey.'

I notice her Louis Vuitton handbag. Of course, Georgia's always had a keen eye.

We make chitchat. I tell her I like her jacket (a lie). 'What, this little number?' she asks.

Her surprise is fake, but I go along with it: I say the gold is gorgeous. I tell her I'm a zoologist and, at this, Louis Vuitton laughs like a kookaburra.

'I love animals,' she says.

'Right.'

'I just looovvvve science.'

I stare at her, mind going blank. 'Drinks!' I shout. 'Can I get you a drink?'

'Darling, red please.'

I back away, and look for Georgia.

She's sweet-talking some lonely ladies. A real opportunist, my Georgia.

'Get back over there,' she whispers. 'You owe me three weeks rent, remember?'

I hadn't forgotten.

'God knows, we need the money,' she says. 'Plus, you're good at this, baby face.'

Yeah, yeah.

'All brown curls and button nose.'

People aren't scared of coming home with me.

I walk over to the folding table in the corner, and order two white wines. Above me, the glass is stained; a few grey fish glide along the bottom, among the weeds and algae. I hand over some gold coins. There's something irreparably sad about grown women drinking out of plastic cups. This must be the seediest pick-up joint in all of New Sydney.

I put on a smile and a happy face, and off I go, back to the lion's den.

'Sorry,' I say returning to Louis Vuitton. I hand her the cup.

'There wasn't red?'

'Oh, shit,' I say. 'Sorry.'

I'm used to ordering white because that's what my ex always drank. The last time we shared a bottle was right before she was taken away.

'No big deal,' she says.

We clink cups.

'Where were we?'

'I think you were talking about your love of dolphins,' I say.

There are maybe a dozen left along the east coast.

While she yammers on, I tune out, but hope I'm creating the impression of being an Active Listener. That's Rule No. 1 in luring cashed-up women home, according to Georgia.

I'd listened to the broadcast last night. 'One for your husband and one for your wife and one for your country,' Top Dog had barked. The population is below replacement level. I threw the radio out the window and it landed with a thunk on the flower hedge.

'…at the Shake and Peck, you know the one … the tips are pretty good…'

So Louis Vuitton was a waitress? But the handbag?

'…and sometimes I go home with the customers…'

Aha. So that's it.

I look over Louis Vuitton's head and see a green sea turtle – short tail, female – hitting her head against the glass. Others gather to look on as the poor creature hurls herself, again and again, against a false hope, a fake sky. This is not the sort of place you take kids anymore – they'd lose all hope in the future. Blood clouds the water. I look away.

Louis Vuitton tells me how she wanted to be a marine biologist as a little girl. When she describes what she imagined her life would look like, I see that she is picturing herself as Ocean Girl. Like in the TV series, she'd wear a torn bikini and talk to whales, and live in underwater stations 'doing science'.

For the first time, I notice her eyebrows are like little furry caterpillars, wiggling up and down with each bland word; they are cute while the rest of her is sharp. So sharp: if all of us here were in the aquarium instead of beneath it, she'd be the Great White (I'd be the clownfish).

'Hey,' I say, 'see that woman over there?'

I'm pointing to Georgia in her sparkly leotard, cross-hatched at the neck. With her red hair and delicate arms she looks like some kind of extinct beetle. Poisonous.

'A bunch of us are going back to ours. Do you wanna come?'

'I'd love to *come*,' she says, baring her teeth.

I wince.

'Fabulous.'

I tell her I'll meet her by the back door in ten.

All I need now is to find someone for me to spend the night with. Orgies aren't my thing, but it's dangerous being on one's own. You never know when the next raid's coming.

I scan the room, land on my new target: a pale, compact woman with blue hair. I make eye contact, smile, then watch as she walks over.

We speed across the overpass, crammed into a maxi taxi, thighs and forearms touching, Georgia up front. She tucks her red hair behind one ear and gives the driver precise directions. It's 3 am. Pop music pulses through the car. Words like 'love' and 'fuck' and 'you' and 'me' get stuck in the air.

I press my face against the window and watch the flickering neon, entire letters and words missing from skylines; Shell becomes hell, and Starbucks, Sucks. The buildings are grey and honeycombed, half-melted into the earth. The blue glow of TVs here and there, but mostly the blocks are pitch-black, abandoned. After the last earthquake, hundreds fled.

A poster on the rump of the bus ahead advertises the aquarium. It looks ancient and worn, the colours faded. Some of the fish are now extinct, the smiling school kids long dead. The gift shop it advertises is still there.

I glance over at Louis Vuitton fixing her make-up. Her lips are red and wet, and she smacks them together, for the mirror, her chin jutting out in challenge.

I whisper to Blue, and she turns to look at me. People like us can sense each other a mile off. It's something about the way we try to minimise the space we occupy, keep our hands to ourselves.

When we pull up to our bunker on Abercrombie, Georgia pays the cabbie and we jump out, one by one, onto the cracked pavement. Louis Vuitton stumbles in her satin stilettos, and I catch a glimpse of her red knickers.

Our place is plastered in graffiti, the windows boarded up. Bits of plastic and paper litter the front porch, including a newspaper that looks a decade old, the corners yellowing, curling. We'd moved here when the earth cracked beneath our old place up on Enmore, and the two bedrooms slid into the dirt. I pick up the newspaper – the mug shot on the cover vaguely resembles someone I used to know.

Still, the air is electric. Even I can sense it.

Two tough-looking women in leather have their arms wrapped around each other. The shorter one has a pistol looped through her belt.

I unlock the door, and step aside to let the others pass.

Georgia leads the way down the corridor, heels clacking like hooves.

'You can leave your stuff here,' she says, pointing to our nice leather couch. 'I have everything we need in my den.' She giggles. 'All the things.'

The ladies hee-haw and drop their bags as directed, except one.

'Aren't you coming?' she asks.

Georgia is quick: 'Jill's got a bit of an infection.'

The ladies give me sympathetic looks.

Georgia winks at me, and the bead curtain twinkles behind her.

'Night, lovies,' she calls.

'I don't really have an infection,' I tell Blue.

'I know,' she says.

We stand still for a moment, watching bodies undress through the iridescent beads. Exposed tits and bits, flat tummies and round tummies, saggy and flabby flesh, strong limbs and weak limbs, hair and no hair, all smiles. One woman has a tattoo of an eel snaking up from ankle to crotch. It's Louis Vuitton.

'Not so fast,' I hear Georgia say in her sweetest voice.

I take Blue by the hand and lead her upstairs. Halfway up, I kick a couple of cockroaches away with my toe.

'Duck,' I shout, as we round the corner.

You have to half-hunch to enter my room, but then, once inside, you can stretch out to your full height, if you're less than five foot six, at least, like me. I crank open the skylight – it's a little rusty – and let in the greenish night. I look out onto the city, blocky and cement-grey, a few scraggy eucalypts, and a rusted-out bus huffing down our street. I miss seeing the stars.

Blue sags onto my futon. 'You have a cat?' she asks, noticing the dark fur.

Why didn't I change my sheets? Most of the cats were, of course, rounded up during the last food crisis.

I shake my head. 'There are possums in the roof.'

I don't tell her I've befriended them.

She glances around at the cardboard boxes along one wall, the rusty heat pipe, and a bottle of half-drunk Absolut.

'Nice place,' she says.

'Yeah, sorry.' I shrug. 'I know it's a dump … but you know what it's like for people like us.'

She nods.

I rinse my hands in the cracked sink – this room, like the den, was once a brothel – and watch the blood from a fresh cut marble the water. I wipe my hands on my tights.

All my furniture is salvaged from the street, or from flatmates. There's hardly anything here that I've spent any money on. I expect everything, always, to be taken away.

Maybe one of Blue's exes was rounded up, too. No reproductive value, no point. All societies need someone to hate – ain't anything personal.

We sit on my bed cross-legged, listening to the prices being negotiated downstairs. Georgia's honeyed voice calls the prices: oral is five dollars per person, and nipple sucks two dollars, two nipples four dollars. If you want to include chocolate sauce or whipped cream, that's another six.

'You wouldn't believe the dry-cleaning costs,' Georgia says, laughing.

We hear the bedsprings squeak as five bodies settle in for business. A shoe is thrown across the floor, a dress unzipped; more laughter.

Blue and I try to ignore it. We play draughts then give each other back rubs. She has a beautiful broad back with prominent shoulder blades like angel wings. It's funny how you can find someone beautiful, but not want to have sex with them. We talk about this a bit.

'Does it ever make you sad?' Blue asks.

'Sometimes.'

I tell her about Anne, how I'd not even seen her being herded into the silver van.

'I was coming back from the shops when I saw the van kicking up dust. By the time I'd realised what was happening, *voom*. Gone.'

Blue's eyes go dark.

I need to keep speaking. 'And her body probably ended up at Johanna Beach.'

'They don't do that anymore. Too far.'

'Where'd you hear that?' I ask.

'Dunno.'

'I drove up there once, you know.'

'To Johanna's?'

'Yeah.'

We lie side by side on my mouldy doona, listening to the groans and moans and shrieks below, some fake, some real; I know the difference. We also hear the neighbours on my left at it, and the neighbours on my right, and some cats fucking on the fence.

'This is so awful. I'm sorry I brought you here.'

A high-pitched squall confirms it.

'It's the same at my place,' Blue says. 'Only maybe worse, because I'm next door to the hospital, and the staff go at it behind the dumpster. Death makes people wanna have sex.'

I tell her I'm sorry again, and hand her some fluffy pink earmuffs. I put on a pair, too. We listen to gunshots in the distance, some whack-job scuffle for space.

Blue rolls over onto her back, belly taut like an apple. I didn't lose the weight after my first surrogacy, maybe that was Blue's trouble, too. Even through the earmuffs, I can hear Blue's belly growl. I pretend our bellies are dugongs chirping and barking to each other in a mating ritual. Of course, the last coral bleaching event wiped them out, too.

The headboard below rattles against the wall, faster and faster. Knock, knock, knock, knock, KNOCK, KNOCK, KNOCK.

I want to howl. I want to be one of the women downstairs, or one of the women outside. I want so much more than this.

The earmuffs aren't doing shit. I pull mine off, then Blue's. I tell her about my role in all of this, making it clear that I'm glad she came round, that she's here, with me, but work's work. What can I do, starve?

'It's a small thing,' I say.

We sneak downstairs and Blue keeps watch at the base of the stairs, while I open and shut the handbags and clutches on the couch. I open the Louis Vuitton, and find a matching wallet with a few fives.

'Jackpot!'

'How much?' Blue asks.

I count twenty-five dollars.

'Sweet Jesus.'

Georgia is going to be stoked.

I unzip a lime green handbag and pocket some gold coins. Something catches my eye at the bottom. Dental dams. Rare, these days. I take those, too, for Georgia. I close the bag and put it back, exactly where it was, between the leopard print and the nondescript black leather.

I think of replacing the radio. Georgia had a near meltdown when we realised the thing was broken (I thought the flower hedge would've softened the landing). 'Why'd you do that for?' she asked in her calmest voice, before hurling a book at my head.

Blue keeps watch like a guard dog, eyes sweeping the room.

'Hurry,' she murmurs, 'someone's coming.'

We hear the ting of the beaded curtains.

I shove the cash in my back pocket, pull Blue towards me. 'Come here,' I whisper. Her tongue feels like a slug in my mouth. Oh, god. She pulls back, wincing.

'Nothing to be shy about, ladies,' the intruder winks.

She's wearing a studded leather harness, and peacock earrings, looking a little like Bettie Page with her black wavy hair. My great-great-grandpa used to have pin-ups of her.

I force myself to smile, and laugh with her.

'Oh, you know!' I say. Then, 'Whatcha looking for?'

'Kitchen. Whipped cream?'

Blue snickers.

'To your left. Cream's on the inside of the fridge door.'

We watch her pockmarked bottom sashay down the corridor.

When she's gone, back behind the beaded curtain, I smile at Blue, tell her I'm sorry about the kiss.

'Don't be,' she says. 'It would've been worse if she'd guessed the truth.'

She's right.

I go through a few more handbags. It's a dirty business. I pocket a Mac lipstick, some Tic Tacs, and a small pack of Oxazepam, and the cash, of course.

'That's my rent money,' I say.

I offer Blue a cut, but she shakes her head.

'I'm not doing too shabbily,' she says.

'What's your secret?'

'I drive the silver vans.'

Something twists inside.

She shrugs, and smiles again.

'Raid, raid!'

It's Georgia's voice.

Words like drumbeats: 'Raid, raid, raid.'

'Grab your things, everyone out!'

I look up at Blue.

Neither of us move.

'Hon, hurry!' someone yells in the next room.

'Oh, fuck, fuck!'

'Where's my shoe?'

We move further inside, towards the kitchen.

'C'mon, everyone out NOW.'

We hear the ladies scramble to collect their things. Someone is crying.

Anne had disappeared just like that, the van kicking up dirt like moon dust.

I motion to Blue and we move to the doorway, where, half-concealed, we can watch the ladies race out the door, some barefoot or with dresses half-zipped.

'Get out of the way!' someone shouts.

We watch the handbags disappear from the couch, one by one.

The two lesbians in leather run out the door holding hands. A frazzled and naked Louis Vuitton jumps down the porch steps, and stumbles out onto the street. The light catches the eel sliding down her leg.

I say nothing.

Blue is chewing her fingernails.

When all the ladies are gone, Georgia flounces into the kitchen wearing nothing but a star-spangled thong, her thighs smeared in whipped cream.

She smiles at us and asks, 'How much?'

The Professional

There's always been a need for people like us. It's just that we're rarely paid. We are the negotiators in our families, the people called in times of crisis, to smooth over differences or hold others to account. We're the ones who plan family holidays. Organise interventions for stray uncles. Take aunts and mothers to medical appointments.

'On behalf of the airline, I would like to extend my deepest apologies for the loss of your luggage. We are doing our best to locate the missing items and will be in touch with you within twenty-one days to provide an update...'

Before I worked for Gizmo Airlines, I waitressed at a pub on George Street where folks elbowed each other to get to the bar, and fights broke out most nights – on the footpath, sometimes inside. I learnt to raise my voice, to be assertive but also kind.

'Sorry, mate, she was here first.'

'Mate, it looks like you've had a bit too much to drink. I'm sorry, I can't serve you.'

I worked the graveyard shift for eight years. Got to know the locals. The tourists, they'd come once and never return. Even made friends with Alexander the Wizard. The guy with the wand that everybody was talking about.

'Pint or schooner?'

Alexander always ordered Resch's in a jug.

In my eighth year of service, I spotted an ad in the local paper for a 'Dispute Resolution Officer'. I almost spat my coffee out. *Of course*, I realised for the first time. *That's me.* Until then, I'd never considered apologising could be a paid vocation.

As the middle child, I'd had plenty of practice smoothing over family tensions. Even held an intervention for Mark when he lost all that money on the greyhounds. Pub work is also great for learning diplomacy.

'One at a time, please.'

'Sorry, we don't do shots after midnight. Can I get you something else?'

After my last shift, a few of us went across the road to another pub. I didn't have to pay for a single drink, and Alexander the Wizard blessed me with his wand, which was a real honour, and tearfully told me to stay safe. On the Monday morning, I put on my new red suit with the blue cravat, and drove to Kingsford Smith Airport.

'We extend our deepest apologies to Gizmo customers for the delay in flights from Sydney to Melbourne today.'

I have a real knack for this stuff. I've been in training my whole life.

Basically, I'm the person you speak to when you call to complain about something. Like lost luggage. Delayed flights. Inadequate in-flight meals, or movies. Flight attendants. Missed connecting flights. Turbulence. Blocked toilets.

'I'm sorry to hear that Gizmo in-flight meals did not meet your expectations on this occasion. I've made a note of your concerns and will pass them on to the head of our catering service.'

It's much easier than working in a pub, that's for sure. I get to sit down, that's a big one. I can pull faces on the phone, even give someone the finger. We have regular breaks. Ten minutes in the morning, half an hour for lunch, and ten minutes in the arvo. And there are travel perks, too. But I haven't made use of those yet.

'On behalf of Gizmo Airlines, I'd like to offer you a flight voucher to compensate for the turbulence you experienced on your Sydney to Beijing flight.'

I apologise for acts of god. For rain and hail. Thunderstorms. Dust storms. A gull sucked into an engine (though perhaps the gull really deserved the apology on that occasion).

'My deepest apologies for the inconvenience you incurred on your recent flight with us.'

In my interview, when the panel asked why I was interested in working for Gizmo Airlines, I gave them my prepared answer.

'I love to travel and understand how important it is to have a comfortable and pleasant journey. I'd like to help others have a good experience, too.'

I haven't actually been overseas. Or interstate. But when I accumulate enough annual leave, I'm going to apply for a stand-by flight. That's when you travel for a small fee when there's a spare seat on a plane. You have to be flexible, but that's easy for me. I've always been pretty adaptable.

I don't know if this is generally known, but you can pick up those glossy brochures from the travel agent for free. I've been collecting them. So far I have: Tahiti, Vanuatu, Fiji, the Maldives and Bali. Bungalows. Palm trees. White sand. Swimming in water so clear you can see your reflection.

I made a vision board for my living room of places I'd like to go. With beach umbrellas and blue lagoons. It's the first thing I see when I leave the house, the first thing I come home to.

'Gizmo Airlines. You're speaking to Kate. How can I help you today?'

'Gizmo Airlines. This is Kate. How can I assist you?'

'Welcome to Gizmo. You're speaking with Kate.'

It's hard to explain to others exactly what I do. I went on a date with a woman who asked what I did for work.

'I say sorry for a living.'

'Sorry?' she said.

'Exactly.'

'What?'

'I'm paid to apologise to customers on behalf of an airline. When things go wrong, like someone's luggage doesn't follow them to their final destination, I'm the person they speak to on the phone.'

Lots of things can go wrong. On one Sydney to Singapore flight, three out of six toilets in economy were blocked, and we had about twenty people ring us afterwards to complain. And fair enough, too.

'On behalf of Gizmo, I'd like to take the time to say how sorry we are that your flight wasn't as comfortable as it could have been.'

It's best not to mention the specifics: faeces, vomit, turbulence. It's too in your face, people don't like it. And it lowers their rating of the airline.

'We'd like to invite you back for a much better experience with Gizmo.'

And so it happened that I rose through the ranks. My apologies became famous. Customers were so satisfied after speaking to me that I rarely had to offer anyone compensation. I saved the company loads of money.

'On behalf of Gizmo Airlines, I'm really sorry about that. How frustrating to receive the Vegetarian Vegan Meal instead of the Vegetarian Lacto-Ovo one you'd ordered. I'll be passing on your feedback to our catering team and can assure you that we at Gizmo are continually trying to improve our services. I hope you will travel again soon and enjoy a more favourable dining experience with us.'

No flight vouchers or points necessary.

When I first started, I'd hear my name called every so often.

'Kate?'

'Yes, Meg.'

My boss snooped on my calls. She had the right – I'd signed a contract that included this clause:

Gizmo Airlines notifies you that it will carry out ongoing, intermittent surveillance of the use of computer systems by you – including emails, phone, internet and files - by all methods available to Gizmo Airlines.

'Kate, don't forgot to use the word *wholeheartedly*. As in, I *wholeheartedly apologise for the inconvenience you incurred*.'

I quickly grasped the situation and formulated a response.

'I'm sorry, Meg. You're right, I have been neglecting to use the word *wholeheartedly*. I'll try to do better from now on.'

I gave her the finger when she wasn't looking.

There's an art to apologising. At Gizmo, we follow The Four Steps to a Personal and Heartfelt Apology:

Step 1. Express remorse
'On behalf of Gizmo Airlines, I would like to offer my heartfelt apologies…'

Step 2. Admit responsibility
'I acknowledge that we failed to deliver…'

Step 3. Make amends

'We'd like to invite you back to make much better memories with Gizmo…'

(If a customer becomes angry or upset, consider offering vouchers, upgrades, points or cash. Speak to your supervisor first.)

Step 4. Promise it won't happen again

'Gizmo takes your feedback seriously. We will do better next time…'

These days I don't need to consciously think about the steps. I can quickly assess the situation, narrow in on the issue, and come up with a response that is personal and sincere. Sincerity is very important. It takes a lot of practice.

Sometimes, it's only the *appearance* of sincerity. Some days, I don't really care if your rissole is under-cooked or your headphones are broken. I have my own problems.

Basically, the ability to deliver a heartfelt apology is a magic superpower. I do it outside of work, too.

When accidentally stepping on someone's foot: 'I'm so sorry. I'm such a klutz. Are you okay?'

When asking the neighbours to turn down their music: 'I'm so sorry to ask, but would you mind turning down the music a touch? I'm an annoying early riser.'

When trying to get off the phone with my sister: 'I'm so sorry, Belle, I really have to run. Doctors can't be kept waiting.'

Belle would stay on the phone for hours given the chance.

'On behalf of Gizmo, I wholeheartedly apologise for the inconvenience you experienced on Flight BA2592.'

'On behalf of Gizmo…'

'On behalf of Gizmo…'

'On behalf of Gizmo.'

Six more months of that and I was promoted to '*Senior* Dispute Resolution Officer'. Alexander the Wizard and I celebrated with a jug of Resch's at my local. He drinks quite a lot of beer for someone so mystical. We've become good friends.

'My sincere apologies…'

'My heartfelt apologies…'

'My wholehearted apologies…'

Some days the work at Gizmo really takes its toll. Not all callers realise that I'm actually *not* the cause of their problems. I didn't personally mislay their luggage or prepare their in-flight meal. I'm a spokesperson for a huge company of 15,000 fallible employees.

On those days, I put my pyjamas on as soon as I walk through my front door. Make myself a mug of hot cocoa and settle on the couch for a night of telly. Sometimes Alexander the Wizard comes over and we watch *MasterChef* together.

I apologise to him, too.

'I'm sorry I'm no fun tonight. It's been a long day. Would you mind if we just watched telly?'

I work 38-hour weeks. I'm always tired. Alexander gets it.

Sometimes, no matter how much of a professional you are, you're unable to resolve a complaint in what's termed a *mutually satisfactory manner*.

Here's a good example.

The man was angry right off the bat. 'This is the third time in as many months that Gizmo has lost my cello.'

'I'm really sorry, Sir.'

'Don't sorry me. I want to be compensated.'

'If your luggage is delayed or missing, Gizmo has twenty-one days to find it and get it back to you. We'll do our best. If we get your luggage back to you within twenty-one days, you can still claim compensation for the delay. If we can't locate your luggage, you can claim for lost luggage.'

'And how am I supposed to play my two gigs this weekend?'

'We recommend that you contact your travel insurer.'

'That's really not good enough.'

'I'm hearing what you're saying, and I will pass on your feedback to our baggage handling team.'

'I'd like to speak to your supervisor.'

Everyone who works in customer service knows that 'supervisor' is the equivalent of 'open sesame'.

'Just a moment, Sir, I'll transfer you.'

Gizmo has a bad track record when it comes to musical instruments. Don't ask me why. Last week, they (or rather 'we') lost a harp, a theremin and a subcontrabass flute. I'd have been more helpful if the man was a tad nicer to me. If you hurt my feelings, I'm not likely to be very helpful.

Meg was seething when she came over to update me. She really wants to be a massage therapist, but that doesn't pay much. In this job, as head of the professional apologisers she earns way more than a schoolteacher.

'I told him we would be happy to pay for the hiring costs of a cello over the weekend.'

'I'm sure he was happy with that,' I said.

'He was a total dick.'

I sympathised with her. She'd been on call 24/7 for three days straight, while the rest of us got to recharge.

'Good afternoon. Gizmo Airlines. You're speaking with Kate!'

The upswing on the 'Kate' helps me set a friendly tone. It tells people immediately that I'm on their side and ready to listen. It's also harder to yell at someone who is being nice to you.

'How can I help you today?'

'Hi there. My name is Mira. I'm wondering if you're a paid professional apologiser?'

We like to keep it on the down low. 'I'm a customer representative,' I tell her.

'Are there any positions going?'

'Not at the moment, I'm sorry.'

'Can you tell me how I can apply for future positions?'

'When there's a vacancy – which only happens very occasionally – we advertise on all the major job boards.'

'What sort of things do they look for?'

'An outgoing personality. Someone who is super positive and intuitive. Intuition is really important.'

I probably said too much. Gave the game away. She insists I take down her contact details 'just in case something comes up'.

Since the *Herald* published that article on profes-sional apologisers at Gizmo we've received more and more calls from people looking for work. As if anyone off the street could do it. It's arrogance, I think. I mean, maybe Mira could do it, but most people couldn't handle it. For one thing, you need a lot of patience and empathy. That was last month and Mira was the last in a long line of job seekers.

Sometimes the calls are what's known as unusual.

'I'm sorry, Sir, that your flight was uncomfortable.'

'Uncomfortable is an understatement. She was topless for eight hours.'

Apparently, the woman sitting next to him removed her top as soon as the plane took off. An exhibitionist, maybe. Or maybe she was over-heating.

'I'm sorry the flight attendants didn't respond to the situation appropriately, Sir.'

'Damn right they didn't.'

'I'm really sorry about that. I'd like to invite you back so you can make better memories on your next flight with us. I'm going to send you a voucher to the value of two hundred dollars to use on your next trip.'

I take note of the flight number in the system and flag the complaint for investigation.

Meg had been listening in.

'Lucky him,' she says. 'Looking at boobs for eight hours. I can think of worse ways to spend my time.'

Me too, actually. But I don't say that.

And to be honest, I think I'm losing my touch. Lately, I haven't been feeling my usual swell of empathy during calls.

Two people on the same flight complained about 'bugs' in their mashed potato. Two more about damaged cabin baggage. A guy called about a crying baby on his long-haul flight. Someone else rang up about a woman who compulsively chewed her blanket and pillow, and then the other passengers' blankets and pillows. I offered that last person an upgrade on their next flight. Which was against company policy, but I just wanted to get him off the phone.

At least I have something to tell Alexander the Wizard when I get off work. He's actually moved in with me. 'We'll live like brother and sister,' he said. And that's basically what's happening. I've divided up the living room with a curtain – couch and telly on one side, Alexander in his fold-out bed on the other. He spends his days casting spells and browsing the glossy travel brochures I bring home. I now also have: Ko Lipe, Hawaii, the Cook Islands. And the Perhentian Islands on the east coast of Malaysia where you can string up a hammock between palm trees.

When I finally get home we sit on the living room floor, cutting out pictures of thatch-roof huts, crystalline lagoons, tropical fish. I even find a photo of Poisson Cru, a traditional Tahitian dish of tuna marinated in lime and coconut milk. Even Alexander says he'd be willing to try it.

'Two more months and I'll have enough leave,' I tell him.

He casts a spell to speed up time. And then we spend two more hours working on my (now 'our') vision board. Nights like these make it easier to get through the next day.

When you pick up the phone, you know immediately if someone's life is on the rocks. Like they're calling not because their flight was unsatisfactory, but because their life is.

'Why is the interior of the plane painted white?'

I'm stumped, but manage to say, 'It's a standard colour scheme, Madam.'

'It feels like you're inside an igloo.'

I want to get her off the phone. It's almost lunchtime and I'm starving.

'Like you're stuck inside a dove. The bird, not the soap, you know?'

'I'm sorry the colour scheme isn't to your liking. I can assure you that we take customer feedback very seriously.'

'What colour will the walls be next time I travel then?'

Oh, what the heck. I take a guess: 'Pastel pink.'

She seems satisfied with that.

Meg berates me for making stuff up. 'What happens when she flies again and finds the walls as white as snow?' she asks.

'Please, no more similes.'

I lose patience even with Meg. The week stretches on.

'Do you know who I am?'

He's probably some CEO or CFO or something.

'Sir, we offer the same level of customer assistance to everyone.'

'I travel every week with your airline, and I've been doing it for decades.'

So have plenty of people.

'The wi-fi was down for five hours,' he tells me. 'Not one, not two. FIVE.'

'I don't know what you'd like me to do,' I say.

'I want an apology and a refund.'

'You can lump it.'

The words leave my mouth before I can register what I've said.

'KATE,' Meg mouths at me.

I hang up the phone in a panic.

'What the hell?' she says. 'And did you just *hang up*?'

'I'm so sorry,' I tell her. 'I panicked. The words just slipped out.'

'This is your final warning, Kate. Take tomorrow off, go for a walk, get some fresh air. Come back with a new outlook on Wednesday.'

So that's what I do. I put on my sandals and catch the bus to Coogee the next day. Alexander joins me there after a séance, and we walk arm in arm along the boardwalk. We see humpback whales in the distance, a cabin cruiser getting too close. The whales are majestic, playing or mating – we're not sure which. Alexander tells me the humpback whale symbolises long-lasting love. Because they mate for life. He tells me to take diaphragmatic breaths at work. I think he cares about me, but also he's keen on a tropical island getaway.

We watch the cabin cruiser steamroll the whales.

On the Wednesday, I turn up to Gizmo Airline Offices with a so-called new outlook. Or so I think.

'Gizmo Airlines. You're speaking with Kate. How can I assist you today?'

'I'm never traveling with Gizmo again.'

'I beg your pardon?'

'I said, I'm never travelling with your airline again.'

'I'm sorry to hear that. Are you able to tell me what happened?'

'The people next to me on the flight were having sex. The *whole* flight. *And* the flight attendants didn't do a thing about it.'

I inwardly sigh.

'I'm really sorry that happened. Could I have your flight number please?'

I make a note in the system.

'They were lesbians.'

'Sorry?'

'Homosexuals. They had their fingers god knows where. Not that I was looking, of course. It was *disgusting.*'

Suddenly I'm plumb out of sympathy.

'I'd like a refund,' she says.

I pretend-type. Clackety-clack. Clackety-clack. 'Just looking it up for you now.' Clackety-clack.

'I've made note of your complaint, and will get back to you with an outcome soon. Thank you *so much* for calling and raising your concerns with us.' I hang up. I know I've missed the mark on sincerity.

'Welcome to Gizmo. I'm Kate. How can I help?'

'You can go fuck yourself.'

'I see.'

I hang up, which is against policy. We have to issue at least two warnings before we hang up.

The guy calls back.

'Go. Fuck. Yourself.'

'That's really original. What are you, eight years old?'

'Go. Fuck. Yourself.'

Instead of hanging up, I tell him to fuck off back.

When I look up, Meg is leaning over me.

'Can we please have a chat?' she mouths.

I hang up and follow her into her office. Photos of her two poodles decorate the walls.

'Look,' she says, 'I know we really want to tell customers to fuck off. But we can't, Kate—

'He told me to fuck off first,' I tell her.

She just looks at me, and I know it's no excuse.

'Our priority is to keep our customers happy. Even if they're dickheads. Even if they're prank callers. You're not setting a good example. I'm really sorry, Kate, but I have to let you go.'

The Four Steps to a Personal and Heartfelt Apology. Meg knows them well.

I've lost my magic power, that much is clear.

I tell her I understand and hope she gets to do the massage therapy course someday. 'By the way,' I add, 'if you're looking for a replacement I can recommend Mira.'

'Who the heck's Mira?'

'Just a friend.'

I jot down her contact details.

With a heavy heart, I log off the computer for the last time. Rinse out my Kermit the Frog mug, and slip it in my handbag, along with my eye drops and the chocolate coins I keep on my desk. I take one last look at the blue cubicles, the rows of headsets, before walking through the sliding glass doors. In the hot, humid air of the Kingsford Smith Airport carpark, I realise I'll never get to Tahiti.

No overwater bungalows, no swimming with turtles, no breadfruit or taro, no hammocks, no pearl farms, nothing. Except, it occurs to me, that Alexander and I could now afford a trip to Brisbane. At least we'll see palm trees, I guess.

Carpark

The sun beats down on their bare heads.

They've been sitting out on the balcony for hours, watching the carpark at the back of a strip of shops. Cars and people coming and going, dogs tied to posts while their owners pick up parcels and cold drinks.

Stace offers Jarred some sunscreen, but he shakes his head. Skin cancer isn't on his mind. He's probably thinking about exams, his dad, whether he has enough money for a Coke.

The baking concrete reminds them of the Kingsford Smith runway.

'Ow!' she yelps. She'd forgotten the table is scorching. 'Who has metal tables?'

'Dad's idea.'

She moves her matching metal chair closer to the railing.

'You could fry an egg on the bitumen.'

Jarred agrees.

The carpark is a stark concrete oblong, surrounded by scarred gums and benches, faded yellow lines marking the car spaces. There's a skip bin by the automatic doors buzzing with flies, black garbage bags spilling out onto the footpath, an empty pink box of Huggies.

They watch people shuffle from their cars to the squat building, and back again.

A schoolgirl clutching a yellow gerbera gets into a Holden, turns the radio up and almost backs into another car before careening down Alice Street. Stace laughs.

Jarred blows smoke into her face. 'Soz,' he says, tapping his ciggie. They'll empty the ashtray outside before his dad gets home.

Stace doesn't smoke, her mum's lungs are bad.

She turns her face away. Maybe they could find some coins behind the couch cushions. Or in the pockets of his dad's overalls. They'd be asking for it, wouldn't they?

They watch a woman in denim cut-offs struggle across the bitumen with her shopping bags. She opens her car boot and just throws them in.

'I hope she hasn't bought eggs.'

'Yeah.'

Even from this distance, it looks like the woman hasn't slept in weeks.

He takes another puff.

So far today they'd watched: a toddler cowering on the ground from a magpie, men in fluoro vests eating meat pies, and some council workers lopping off tree branches grown too close to the powerlines. Plenty to see.

Stace notices something else. 'Look.'

'Where?'

'Under the banksia. *There.*'

Jarred squints into the sun.

Two boys in school uniform are having a pash.

'Good for them,' he says, surprising her.

She'd expected the usual macho crap.

'Wish I had someone to kiss,' she says.

'You can kiss me.'

'F-off.'

They'd met each other at one of those stupid co-ed school dances, but they didn't like each other like *that*, though they sometimes pretended they did. It made it easier for them at school, especially for Jarred.

'My dad thinks we're a couple,' he says.

'I don't care.'

They watch as the tall boy takes the other's hand and he smiles and says something. They clasp their mouths together again. And then, just as quickly, the shorter one is climbing down the grassy verge, leaving the other leaning against the tree trunk, watching him go.

'Someone's gonna beat them up,' Jarred says.

'What about marriage equality?'

The bill has only just been passed.

'You don't know shit, Stace.'

She knows that Jarred's dad beats him up.

'Whatever.'

She also knows Jarred likes boys, even though he's never said anything to her.

Why hasn't she brought her hat? Her scalp is burning. She slaps some more sunscreen on her forehead. 'You want some?'

'Nah.'

Stace observes the boy, now sitting on the grass, unzipping his schoolbag. He pulls out a notebook and a pen, probably to do some homework. She'd practised on oranges, but would like to kiss someone IRL. Maybe Benjie in geography.

A postie in a floppy hat stops at the locked metal box beside the carpark and slips its contents into her trolley. Mostly wads of letters held together with elastic bands and a few parcels.

'So that's what they're for.' Stace has always thought those slim, army-green boxes had something to do with electricity.

'Yeah.'

He's probably seen everything from this balcony. Fights, car crashes, kids tagging the brick.

The postie pulls the tarp over the mail like a mum with a baby blanket. They watch her trundle down the street towards Myrtle Lane.

Maybe she could be a postal worker.

'You hungry?' Jarred asks.

'What have you got?'

'Cheese, bread.'

'Sounds good.'

She never brings food to school, scabs money off the other kids, twenty cents, fifty cents, a dollar if she's lucky.

They go inside, the interior dark and shadowy.

'I can't see shit,' Jarred says, flicking on the light.

They bang around in the cupboards and fridge.

He arranges two slices of Bega on two plates with multigrain and half a wrinkly tomato. 'That okay?'

'Great. You got sauce?'

'Barbecue?'

As soon as they bring their plates outside, the corners of the cheese start to melt.

'Look at that,' she says. 'Sun-grilled sandwiches.'

The cheese is salty and delicious. She's starving, but too polite to say anything. If her mum taught her anything, it was good manners.

He can't take his eyes off the tall boy. Brown hair catching the sun, angular body bent over schoolwork. She's thinking, if he could concentrate like that at school maybe he'd be doing better.

'You okay?' she asks.

'Yeah. Why?

'No reason.'

He rubs his bicep.

'Must be hitting the forties.'

'Yeah.'

Both sense the growing menace in the air. You can't escape the heat. But still there are the usual things to do: errands to run, kids to feed and pick up from school, homework, dishes to wash, dogs to walk, groceries to buy.

Below them, a woman in shorts crosses the carpark with a black garbage bag.

Jarred takes another mouthful. 'Think it's a chopped-up body?'

'Yeah. Her husband's.'

The woman swings it into the bin, looks left and right.

'Dodgy as.'

'I bet it's like industrial waste.'

'How come?'

She tells him what she'd read in the paper about businesses illegally chucking chemicals into skips.

'Cheap fucks.'

They've polished off their cheese and bread.

'You want some more?'

She knows there's nothing left in the fridge. 'Nah, I'm good, thanks.'

He refills their glasses from the kitchen tap, comes back outside.

The fireball-sun dips in the sky, but the temp won't drop for a few more hours. She pictures skin cells multiplying like on that ad with girls in bikinis. Her bum is sticking to the seat.

A P-plater skids to a stop at the lights.

'Probably Mum's Ford Ranger.'

'Yeah.'

Someone's telly is tuned to *Jerry Springer*, which Stace thinks is the best show in the world.

'It's stupid.'

'I like to watch it with Manda,' she says, 'when she's in town.' Her sister mostly stays away.

It's too stinking hot to be watching telly. They can hear the angry voices from here. Someone accusing someone of something or other.

She's thinking of Damien's mouth. Cherry-pink bow. Chapstick lips. She knows he made out with Jarred behind the soccer pitch, before his mum pulled him off the team.

When he finishes his dad's pack of Horizons, he moves his chair closer to Stace. They sit like that, arms draped over the balcony railing, watching the world go by. There's lots to see if you bother to look. Like where do the seagulls come from? They're forty kilometres from the sea. She watches them soar above the faded shop awning, dip down to peck at chips and rubbish, squawking and screeching like hangry kids.

The carpark starts to fill up as school finishes for the day, and they watch kids join the queue at Charlie's Chicken. The tall boy is still there, reading under the tree, oblivious to the cars whooshing past, kids clutching greasy paper bags, laughing and shouting, their cans of soft drink sweating in the sun.

'I could go a Coke.'

'Yeah.'

'Dad's gonna be home soon. Wanna go to Charlie's?'

It was always a good idea to be gone before Mr Boosalis got home. He had a temper that flared and shrivelled, the damage done in seconds (like the sun in that government-sponsored ad).

Jarred checks his wallet. 'I've got like six bucks. You?'

She looks at the coins in her palm. 'Three, four? Five bucks.'

'Alright.'

He empties the ashtray into the outside bins, while she washes up their plates. She pushes the tomato stalk down the sink. They know how to erase all traces. To move like ghosts through space.

As she's wiping the crumbs off the metal table, there's a shout from the carpark.

'Jarred!' she calls.

A group of boys is taunting someone.

'Jarred, look.'

He leans over the railing next to her. 'That's the boy…'

'The one under the tree?'

'Yeah.'

A man with a walking frame glances at the teenagers before upping his pace and disappearing behind the glass doors.

'He looks scared.'

'Wouldn't you be?'

They can't hear the words but they feel the aggression. There are six or seven of them, half in school uniform.

'Fuck. What if they really hurt him?'

He looks deflated. 'Fucking idiots.'

The boys are closing in and one of them swings a punch.

'Why isn't anyone doing anything?'

The carpark is full of people.

'People are fucking shits.'

They recognise faces from Jarred's school. A kid called William and his sidekick Johnny, Noah with the cauliflower ear, a few others from the year above.

'Reckon we should call the police?' she asks.

'Someone probably has.'

'What if they haven't?'

Johnny smacks his fist into the side of the boy's face. Stace knows he wears rings: the boy's face will be tenderised like a fillet of beef. Another kid chucks a Coke can at the boy.

Even from up here, they can hear the jeers, the word *faggot*.

The tall boy sways with the punches. The boys are hyenas.

Stace leans over the railing, looks up then down, to the side. 'Jarred, look, they're all watching.'

The neighbours have come out to watch from their balconies. Even the sullen Mr Reilly.

She turns to look at him. 'We need to call the police, now!'

'I'm sure someone already has.'

'Seriously, what if they haven't?'

As the boy slumps to the ground, they lose sight of him. All they can see is a scrum of kids swinging their school shoes. Some passing girls in school uniform look on, before joining the queue at Charlie's.

'Fuck, Jarred, if you don't do it, I will.' She disappears inside and comes out with the cordless.

'Give it here,' he says.

He doesn't need to look up the number of the local police. Knows it off by heart.

'Hello, hello,' he's saying into the receiver. 'Someone's being beaten up pretty bad … in the carpark outside Noreen Street, outside the mall.'

'Hurry up,' Stace is screaming. 'They're killing him. Fuck, Jarred. The little shits are killing him.'

He raises his hand. 'Shut up. I can't hear what she's saying … Corner of Noreen and Boundary. Near the playground. North side, on the grass.' He grabs Stace's arm, makes her face him. 'They're on their way.'

The jeers and slurs are rising up from the baking concrete and even though she can't make out the words, she knows they won't stop till they've killed him.

He hangs up the phone, drops it on the table.

Stace juts her head out over the railing, screams at the neighbours. 'Why the fuck didn't any of you do something? Can't you see what's happening?'

Blank faces look back at her.

'They saw everything that happened, that's why,' Jarred answers.

They can't look away. It's too horrible. She wants to say something comforting, but what?

'Are you crying?'

'F-off,' he says.

At last, they hear sirens in the distance, and the boys, hearing them too, scramble down the grassy verge, scattering like marbles, as the ambos swerve into the carpark, followed by the blue and white of the police.

They have a clear view now: the boy spreadeagled on the concrete. A puddle of blood around his head, red-brown tracks made by the attackers' shoes.

'He's not moving, Stace.'

Car doors slam and then the two paramedics are crouching on the ground. Their thick bodies shield the boy. The police move more slowly. Onlookers gather with shopping bags and cold drinks.

'Where the fuck were all you fuckers before?'

She pulls Jarred into a hug, and he leans against her, watching as the boy is lifted onto the stretcher.

'Do you think he's gonna be okay?'

'Who knows?'

Two officers stand around the brown puddle, one of them jots something down. The ambulance speeds towards the highway.

'Just 'cos he likes boys.' She lets the words hang, but he's already turning away—

'Dad's home.'

She strains to hear feet on the stairs.

Already, the sirens have faded into the distance. It's like nothing's happened, all the neighbours inside, behind closed doors, watching the telly now there's nothing to see outside. Some gulls pick at the hot chips left by the boys.

She picks her schoolbag off the ground.

'Hi, Dad,' Jarred calls from the balcony. 'Stace's here.'

The sheer bulk of Mr Boosalis always surprises her. He's squat like a washing machine, and strong.

He pokes his head outside. 'Hey, Stace, my favourite girl.' His smile is forced. 'Why don't you kids get some fresh air? I'm beat.'

'Sure, Dad. We're just on our way out.'

They grab their bags and call out bye, but Mr Boosalis is already opening a beer. They jog down the stairs, turning away from the red-brick block, heading towards the grim-faced police officers with notebooks.

'I'm gonna give them some names,' Jarred says, as they walk towards the glistening pool of blood on the bitumen.

Landlord in the Attic

Our ramshackle terrace in Redfern, shared by seven, is falling apart, quite literally. The kitchen ceiling collapsed last week, squashing the chairs and table flat. Adam took photos of the damage and called it A Work of Art. Whorls of black mould decorate the walls, and everything leaks and stinks like damp laundry hung up inside too long. The wind is battering the windows and walls. It's been raining non-stop for forty-two days.

Ellie, we need two more buckets, Lakshi tells me.

There aren't any, I say, sipping my tea at the kitchen counter.

What?

THERE ARE NO MORE BUCKETS.

Oh, for fuck's sake.

Here, use *this*. I hand Lakshi an old, charred saucepan.

Ellie! Why don't you make yourself useful!

You know I'm not good in emergencies, I say.

It's true. I panic whenever called upon to apply first aid or dial triple zero. I'm also a perfectionist so I avoid doing anything I suspect I might not get right.

Well, make me a cup of tea then, Lakshi snaps.

Sure.

I will the kettle to boil with my eyes. Nothing happens. People are always demanding too much.

Where's my tea, El?

I'm moving out of this shithole, I say to no-one in particular.

We're always threatening to leave, every time something breaks.

Jim Beam strides into the kitchen, his hair a wet tangle, looking real mad. I can only assume he hasn't managed to patch the roof up outside.

I'm moving out, he says.

Oh, yeah? Where would you go?

John's living under the bridge. I could join him, he says, It's gotta be drier than this rat hole. They got this bonfire and they roast those purple potatoes – you know the ones. And they drink water straight out of the harbour.

He means the Harbour Bridge. The Minister has decked out the underside with portaloos and blue tarpaulins. And if you donate bone marrow every month, no-one bothers you much.

Jim, you'd get sick of potatoes, I say.

Nikki, walking into the kitchen, agrees with me. She's wrapped in a blue bath towel, the bobby pins in her hair jutting out like spikes.

New hole, she says, pointing upward.

This is what I mean. That hole's the size of a tomato, Jim says, indignant.

We all come and stand beside him.

I wring water out of my dress into the nearest bucket, faded red, cracked, older than my mother.

Ellie, where the fuck's the tea at?

It's coming. I drag myself over to the sideboard and press the kettle button. I don't really have telekinetic powers, though I like to make out I do. I measure out two heaped teaspoons of *Cheer Up, Sunshine* and pour boiling water into the teapot.

Ellie, could you pass a cup? Nikki asks.

The one with the kangaroo okay?

I want the Scrabble mug.

H for Harry or G for Godiva?

Cheer Up, Sunshine was a gift from Flo, my ex-girl-friend. It's green tea with a smattering of guarana berries, or something like that. What have you got to be sad about? Flo used to say. Well, there's my depres-sion, I'd remind her. Oh *that*, she'd say.

One day, when Flo was at work, I chucked her stuff out the third-floor window and watched the neighbours fossick for knick-knacks, shoes and leather. A teenage girl with an undercut made off with Flo's vintage pair of Jeffrey Campbells. I laughed behind the curtains.

While I sip my tea and reminisce, the others plug up the holes in the walls with old rags. A bit here, a bit there. I shout: *Plug it up! Plug it up! Plug it up!* I'm thinking of poor bleeding Carrie, of course. Nikki tells me to shut it.

This next rag's going in your mouth, babe, she says.

She doesn't get my humour.

Afterwards, we crawl into Clara's bed and put on our respirators. The green air-purifiers, cheaply made, leave imprints on our pale, papery skin. We look like giant, carnivorous insects. Better that than inhaling toxic fumes, though.

I spot some strange rust-coloured spots fanning out from one corner of the doona. Honey II wriggles in and pokes her little nose out, resting her face on my shoulder.

A few weeks ago, the eaves outside my bedroom window were torn off by the wind, landing on the footpath below, rusty nails pointing skyward. I ran out in my bathrobe, my boobs poking out, and saw a mangled paw peeking out from beneath the timber.

My rotting eaves had squashed Honey I.

The whole street turned out for the funeral, including the nasty Wilson children who used to throw pebbles at Honey. Lakshi said a few words, so did Adam, and I served pickled onions and frankfurts. When Mr Wilson complained about my catering, I socked him and told him to Respect The Dead. Someone called the police and that was the end of poor Honey's wake.

Honey II licks me, and for a moment she looks just like the first Honey. But what do I know. My eyes are streaming from the dust and mould and whatever other toxins thrive here. I might even be allergic to the cat.

Shove over, will ya? Jim Beam is always complaining about falling off the mattress.

You shove over.

Tuck your knees in, I say, helpfully.

Nikki's underarms smell like damp forest, and I nudge her in the ribs. Shove over, I growl.

We shower every second day, except Nikki, who has a water phobia. At the moment, with the help of Clara (a trained-now-unemployed psychologist), she can comfortably look at a teaspoon of water.

Nikki, please, I say, have a bath tomorrow, okay?

Piss off, Ellie.

We have a version of this conversation every night.

In the morning, Louie the landlord pays us a visit. Since the rains started, Louie has become a grey-haired fixture in our home, pottering around, painting this, painting that. The superficial 'improvements' seem bizarre, given the prospect of another collapsed ceiling and so we start to suspect he plans on selling the place. We know lots of other desperate students, immigrants and creative types who would love to get their hot little hands on a shithole like this.

Louie likes to do all the repairs himself; it's his special brand of cost reduction. He mixes my name up and raises my blood pressure. Clara says this is no good for me – he makes me violent. Usually, we do some breathing exercises and knock down trees with baseball bats. This helps, a little.

Been living here long, love? Louie asks, when I open the door.

Oh 'bout six years, I say, rolling my eyes.

Hannah, isn't it?

I'm Ell-ie.

No need to be cranky, love.

If he calls me love one more time, I might just snap his rubber-chicken neck. But I don't want to upset Clara. While he disappears upstairs, I make another batch of *Cheer Up, Sunshine*. Honey II jumps on my lap and we talk about our Plans For The Future. I tell Honey to get out while she still can.

Follow your heart, I say.

She snickers.

Out of the two us, the cat has more sense.

Hannah? Louie calls, coming down the stairs.

It's Ell-ie.

Come look at the windowsills. They look real nice.

I follow his watermelon bum up the narrow stairs. I wonder how many regular-sized bottoms might be made from his rump. At least six or seven. Maybe eight. He tells me how lucky I am to have a landlord like him.

If you had a different landlord, you wouldn't be so lucky, he says.

You're a regular Mother Teresa, I tell him.

Our front door is rotting and splintering, mushrooms grow in the corridor, and when we shower we take a saltshaker with us to ward off the leeches. I don't need to be told how lucky I am.

I wonder why he's painted the windowsills. The windows rattle and the glass has come clean off the pane – dash of paint won't do anything. And what was wrong with natural wood, anyway?

He spreads his arms out.

Ta-da!

The glass is smeared with fresh white paint and my bedroom floor is covered in little flakes of what, optimistically, could be said to look like snow.

When Louie is out of earshot, I curse him to hell.

The fucker has painted my windows shut.

In spring, we fumigate. We are on first-name basis with our pest-control guy, the sweet-natured Jordan. We call him for rats, roaches, bird mites, ants, termites, spiders and those new-generation insects that are a cross between turtles and black widow spiders.

He brings me red roses and those sticky caramels in heart-shaped boxes. When I protest, he tells me I don't need to reciprocate his love.

Let me love you, he says.

(Seeing as how others aren't falling over themselves to love me, sure, okay.)

But just for now, until I find someone else, I tell him.

Jordan agrees.

Flowers are hard to come by these days. I know they're expensive. I mean, look, you could be saving for a little studio in some concrete bunker in Wolli Creek, I tell him. You'd have enough money for a deposit in … twenty, maybe twenty-five years.

The roses stop arriving on my doorstep after that.

In summer, our cramped terrace heats up like a pizza pocket. There's no cross-breeze, no air-con, and when we pass each other in the corridor, our torsos stick together.

The heat is driving us batty. It's all we can talk about.

I've never been so cranky or violent, I hate everyone and everything, my mum is coming to visit so we have to tidy this dump – she makes me so, so nervous – Nikki still hasn't washed, and Jim Beam has drunk all the fucking bourbon, and there's no ice, anyway.

When Louie comes to the door on Monday to demand the rent, I'm *already* pretty wound up and I hit him over the head with a saucepan.

There's a hollow klang and he slumps forward onto the lino.

Fuck, Ellie!

Nikki is screaming.

What are you doing?

Is he dead?

I roll him over. Nope. Come on – let's tie him up.

And put him *where*? Nikki asks, turning a lovely radish-pink.

What about my room? I say. He might like the freshly painted windowsills.

I'm trying to take more initiative – and I think it's paying off. No-one questions my behaviour, not even Clara. This does worry me a little.

We hide Louie in the draughty attic above my room, and slip pieces of toast between the wooden slats.

We don't pay rent anymore and everyone agrees this arrangement is a big improvement. The only person who objects on moral grounds is Jim Beam – and so he moves under the Harbour Bridge. A week in, he dies of dengue.

At first I feel bad about keeping Louie locked up but now that we've settled into a routine of sorts, even Louie seems to be enjoying himself. He's even started on renovations, put in some plumbing, strung some fairy lights between the rafters.

Sometimes we visit him. We squeeze ourselves in between broken springs on the miniature couch and sprawl on his dusty floor.

You know, it isn't so bad here, Louie says, examining the new carpet we give him. It's one of those old faded Turkish rugs that some of our grandparents had but covered in mildew. We tell Louie we can't spare anything else.

You're lucky to have a carpet at all, we tell him. And we believe it. He is lucky to have people like us.

I'm not complaining. I like it here, fewer responsibilities. Plus my night vision's improved, Louie tells us.

For his fiftieth birthday, we take the smoke detector off the wall, and light up a Betty Crocker like a warzone. We even get him a cat, Honey III.

I take Flo back and together we look after Louie in the attic. Because we no longer have to pay rent, Flo and I get to eat out once in a while and even buy warm clothes and proper rain gear. Flo buys a new pair of ridiculously high Jeffrey Campbells. We book flights to Tasmania. Most of the population there live underground, in a network of burrows, surviving on mushrooms and grubs.

It's poverty tourism, I complain to Flo.

Babe, it's all we can afford. You want to go on a holiday or not?

This is so fucked.

Flo and I decide to get married on our return. Louie has started seeing another rehabilitated landlord, a Mr Hockie, and in the spirit of generosity we invite him and Louie to the wedding, along with Clara and Nikki and Lakshi and Adam and Harry and Godiva. We make an effigy of Jim Beam and prop him up against the bar – he would've loved that. We wear tuxedos and drink bourbon, and make merry until curfew.

It rains every day now. Flo's eggs have shape-shifted into sperm, thanks to New Developments in Science. We have children, first one then two and three, and so continue the sordid cycle of life. Louie is our kids' godfather, and we let him out of the attic for each birth. He seems to appreciate it, and we appreciate him.

Picket Fence

As we drove up to our new rental, the boot bulging with our stuff, we saw an old woman squatting on the nature strip. 'Is she taking a shit?' Tilly asked.

'Yep, looks like it.'

The woman was wearing a loose blue housedress that clung to her thighs. She gave us a quick wave as we parked beside her and then she disappeared, across the road, into Number Twelve. That was our introduction to the neighbourhood.

'I think we'll like it here.'

Tilly laughed.

Our new house was a boxy fibro painted sky-blue with a white picket fence. One big room, bedroom off to the side, a small toilet. White window frames, white door. The flowerbeds overgrown. Thistles and scorched grass. 'I'm gonna fix them up,' I told Tilly. 'Plant some freesias.' The lawn needed mowing, too.

She unpacked our clothes while I washed and put away the crockery. Most of the stuff had come from Vinnies or from Ma. We had fold-out camping chairs for the living room, a crate for a coffee table. Tilly promised we'd buy a couch soon. 'First pay cheque.'

I didn't mind, I told her. 'It reminds me of our early camping trips. Sleeping by the creek, eating tinned spaghetti. The lingering smoke of mosquito coils.'

We'd been unpacking for hours when Tilly called a beer break. 'They're in the esky.'

Home-brewed, a gift from her brother. I'd always liked Ben. He looked out for us when others didn't. Funny man, squat and balding with a boyish smile. I knew I'd miss him.

Tilly was sitting on the front steps. 'Look at the stars. They're bright tonight.'

I opened our beers. 'And the silhouettes of the sassafras trees. I think we'll be okay here, dove.'

'Either way, the sky's pretty.'

The couple in the house opposite had the lights on, curtains open, and we watched them strip off for bed. The Shitter's house, a few doors down, was already dark.

I brought out some more of Ben's beers.

*

We were alphabetising our book collection when the commotion started. 'Hey! Stop!' someone was yelling. I ran outside to see the Shitter chasing after a hulking teenager in denim.

'She's got my wallet,' the Shitter howled.

I bolted after the girl, my bare feet slapping the pavement.

'Hey!' I yelled. 'Hey! At the very least take the money but throw the wallet back, okay!'

The girl hesitated. She fumbled then tossed the wallet over her shoulder.

'Thank you!'

We watched her disappear around the bend.

Tilly said, 'Well done. That was some fast thinking.'

'Thank you,' the Shitter added.

I nodded. 'How much did she take?'

She opened her wallet. 'A couple of twenties.'

Tilly and I wondered what kind of hellhole we'd fallen into.

'People used to come here to ride the – whatsit?' I asked once we were back inside.

'The Zig Zag Railway. The place used to be called Scenic World. There was that aerial cable car, remember? The biggest in the Southern Hemisphere.'

'I think I remember.'

We were up to the M's now. Malouf, Marquez, Marsden, Martel.

'Must've been a decade or more ago. Scenic World went bust,' Tilly was saying. 'There's no money here anymore. You can see it on people's faces… What's her name?'

'The Shitter?'

'Yeah.'

'Dunno, but I reckon she would have done okay back in the day. Till … do you think she's trying to scare us off?'

'Like a reverse Neighbourhood Watch?'

'Something like that.'

After Tilly stopped laughing, she conceded it might be true. 'Who knows?'

I spent the afternoon pulling out the weeds between the pavers. It was tough on the knees but gratifying.

*

'Go get 'em!' I yelled, and Tilly grinned as the screen door banged behind her. I could tell she was scared though. I'd been out of work for so long, I couldn't imagine starting someplace new, starting from scratch.

I decided to cook hunza pie for dinner as a treat. The food co-op was a fifteen-minute walk uphill, and when I stepped inside it was empty except for two shoppers who knew each other. One of them was wearing red sandals. I felt my skin prickle as they glared at me.

I handed over some gold coins and said two words to the cashier.

'Have a nice day,' she said, looking over my head.

The streets here were leafy and hilly – no wonder I hadn't seen any joggers. Maybe I'd get a shopping buggy, make it easier for myself. Was I too young? I didn't think so.

As I was crossing the street, I caught a glimpse of the Shitter talking to someone in the shade. Getting closer, I realised it was the teenager. The girl who'd stolen her wallet!

'You!' I yelled.

The girl shrugged.

She was wearing red board shorts and a tight singlet. We were miles from the nearest beach.

The girl turned to the Shitter. 'Be seeing you.' She waited for a white ute to drive past before crossing the road.

'Did you get your money back?' I asked, confused.

She grinned.

She was wearing a jaunty little hat with a blue feather that waved in the breeze.

'Okay then, bye,' I said, turning away.

The Shitter was either batshit crazy or pretending to be.

The sun scorched my bare shoulders as I trudged up the hill with the shopping. Dragonflies and butterflies flitted between bright flowers, but my thoughts stayed with the Shitter. I hitched up my shopping and kept going. The instant I turned into our leafy street I knew something was off. As I got closer, I couldn't believe my eyes.

'Fuck.'

Someone had spray-painted our white picket fence.

A thick black wave from left to right. I dropped the shopping and stared.

Go away, the black line said. *You're not welcome.*

While I was standing there paralysed, the Shitter caught up with me. 'They did your

fence, too, then?' she said in an almost-normal tenor.

'You know who they are?'

'Everyone knows,' she said, enigmatically, before loping away.

I decided she must have a screw loose.

I marched straight back into town and into the hardware store. I wanted to fix this before Tilly got home. There was no need to upset her.

Going for the black line with the roller, I scanned the street for possible culprits. I did the valleys with a brush. While I waited for the first coat to dry, I kept guard under the shade of the old banksia. Ben's beers kept me company.

'Julian, get back here!' a girl was shouting. 'Get back here.' A little kid was pointing at something in the grass.

'Poo,' he said. 'Big poo.'

I laughed, suspecting the Shitter.

'It's probably a big dog,' the girl said, pulling her brother away.

I ducked inside to grab another beer before resuming my guard-dog duties. I suspected the Shitter was responsible for the graffiti. And maybe the teenage girl. They were in on something together, I was sure.

Tilly had had a rubbish day, too, it turned out. She told me about it in between mouthfuls of hunza pie. 'This is really great by the way … what's in this? Silverbeet?'

'Yeah.'

'So the kids were running around, screaming, falling off their chairs. One kid brought a power drill from home. A power drill! He took out the screws from the cupboard doors.'

'Jesus, Till.'

'Little turd. He sure knew how to use it though!'

'I guess you should thank his parents for that.'

She laughed.

'What are you going to do,' I asked, 'about the kids?'

'No idea. Pray they behave themselves? Who knows? Maybe you'll get a job and I can stay home for a while.'

'You know that's unlikely.'

I'd been on disability support for half my life.

'Why don't we get up on the roof?' I suggested.

There were cigarette butts around the chimney from previous tenants.

'The sky's pretty, huh?' Tilly said.

We watched the grey clouds chase each other.

'Look! That one looks like a dragon. No, not a dragon – a bunny. Does that look like a bunny to you?'

'Hah, I don't know, Till. Maybe?'

While the bats clicked in the fruit trees, I told her about the graffiti. And the teenage girl talking to the Shitter.

'You suspect them?' she asked.

'Who else?'

'Why would they be trying to scare us off?'

*

I had another run-in with the Shitter, this time at the food co-op. She was stuffing the pockets of her housedress with wrinkly pears. 'You can't do that,' I whispered. She pushed past me, through the plastic strip curtain.

'She's known to the police,' the teenager at the till said. 'They can't do anything, but. Connections, you know?'

I nodded and backed out of the store.

How long before I understood the rules here?

While I was admiring a crocodile-shaped letterbox, I noticed the Shitter again. She was squatting on the grass, rocking back and forth.

'You really like the nature strips, huh?'

She grinned.

'You know, the people who live in that house—'I pointed behind her '—are probably using their dog's poo bags to scoop up your shit.'

She frowned.

'So one of their rugrats doesn't step in it,' I added.

'That'll teach them.' She hitched up her underwear. 'Yes, siree!'

'Teach them what?'

'That the town doesn't belong to them.'

Her eyes for once were bright and clear.

I spent the afternoon pulling thistles out. I assembled our compost bin, watered the garden. For dinner

I cooked asparagus and eggs in mornay sauce. When Tilly asked me what it was, I told her it was Ma's old recipe (it was actually from Taste.com) – I'd spent too long in the garden.

'I think she's acting crazy to scare us off,' I told Tilly, over dinner. 'Doesn't like newcomers or change or something.' I was speculating. 'Maybe she's one of those types that wants to restore the town to its former glory.'

'Or a xenophobe.'

'Maybe.'

When we finished our beers, Tilly offered to do the dishes, but I pushed her away. 'I've got them, hon.' I wanted to prove my usefulness. Didn't want Tilly suggesting I get a job. 'You go rest.'

*

On Friday night, there was a party a few doors down. Uni students, we thought. Milk crates out the front, rusty bikes. We fell asleep to what Tilly identified as House music

'Why's it called that?'

'Because you play it indoors, I think, at home,' she said.

It was probably the music my sons had listened to when they were that age.

Doof-doof-doof.

I woke up to Tilly poking me in the ribs. 'Get up!'

'What? What's happened?'

'Get up, hon.'

And then we were standing barefoot on the lawn, and I couldn't believe what I was

seeing. Half our fence was gone. The party-goers had stolen the pickets.

'The little weasels!'

I marched down the street in bare feet. 'Hey!' I called, banging on their door.

'Anyone up? Hey!' I knocked until I heard footsteps.

'What?'

The guy's blond hair was damp and limp. He kept sucking his teeth.

'Yeah?' he said.

'You damaged my fence.'

'No, we didn't.'

I swept my arm behind me. 'What are *our* pickets doing on *your* lawn then?'

He scratched his head.

'You owe me a fence, buddy.'

Apart from our white chipped boards, other objects were strewn across their

overgrown lawn: car tyres, empties, bongs, an inflatable kiddie pool.

I remembered the graffiti. 'Did you guys spray-paint our fence on Monday?'

'You should ask Marjorie about that.'

'Who's she?'

'Wears muu-muus and shits on everyone's lawns?'

'Why would she spray-paint my fence?'

'She doesn't like newcomers.' He sucked his teeth again. 'I wouldn't put it past her, is what I'm saying.'

The kid was probably telling the truth.

'Okay, but you still owe me a fence.'

*

Coming back from our bushwalk to Echo Point, Tilly noticed it first.

'How weird.'

An envelope stuck out of our letterbox.

'On a Saturday?'

We opened it right there in our driveway.

The letter from the students was typed on A4 paper. Although they didn't graffiti our fence, they did pinch our pickets, it said. They offered to pay for a new one, but also warned us that *theft and property damage are not uncommon in this area.*

'They're trying to scare us off, too.'

'But look at those well-structured paragraphs,' I marvelled. 'Lawyers in the making.'

We kept reading.

The letter ended with, *Marjorie is well known for her antics in town. She likes to put on a show for newcomers. The last tenants at your house hid on the roof when Marjorie really got going.*

'That would explain the cigarette butts.'

'Marjorie's definitely a nutbar.'

'Maybe,' Tilly said, 'but the town's behind her.'

We refused to admit defeat.

While Tilly was at work, I pulled the pickets out and stacked them ready for council pick-up. From the hardware store, I'd picked up fifty metres of indestructible fencing from a sullen guy in a red vest. 'Toughest stuff we have.' I spent hours in our front yard. The sweat poured down me like water from a bucket. As I was packing away my tools, the Shitter came by – of course she did.

'Emu wire.' She surveyed my handiwork.

I'd sealed our entire block in the heritage wire mesh.

'Impossible to graffiti,' she said.

I stared. 'What would you know about graffitiing?'

Marjorie grinned. 'Not a thing.'

'Yeah, right.'

She grinned again.

By the time I'd cleaned up, Marjorie was fertilising the roses across the road.

'Watch out for those thorns!' I called out cheerfully. I hoped she pierced a buttock. What was wrong with this town? With these people?

When Tilly's car crunched up the drive, I ran down to meet her.

'Nice work,' she said, looking at the fence. 'Landlord will be happy.'

'This stuff's indestructible.'

*

The next afternoon when I came home, the emu wire was half ripped out. It looked as though Marjorie and her Reverse Neighbourhood Watch had taken a chainsaw to it. There were holes big enough for a pony to jump through.

'You little shits,' I screamed at the empty street. 'You shitheads!'

I saw a curtain flicker in the house opposite. They were watching me disassemble. I'd had it!

'You little shits!' I screamed again.

I marched to the Shitter's house at Number Twelve and pulled my underpants down.

I had to strain a little, my face burning. When I crossed back to our house, I knew I'd sunk to a new low. This was exactly what the town wanted.

Without stopping to think, I packed up the whole house, locked the doors and windows, and waited in the driver's seat for Tilly to get home. I'd had enough of small towns and shitters. I wanted to move to a big anonymous city where no-one knew each other, and you might be dead for days before anyone noticed. Yes, that sounded perfect. I picked up my phone and dialled Tilly's number. 'Where are you, dove?

Big Ted

Marie's current patient was an amputee, and she was performing a miracle. Reattaching the severed arm with thread. 'That's Big Ted,' his owner, the girl in pigtails, had told her. She'd been crying, poor thing, when she'd come into the shop.

Marie always made a point of enquiring about injuries. 'Did he have a fall, sweetie?' she'd asked directly but kindly. The girl's mother had intervened. 'He's had a bit of an accident, that's all. We couldn't get here sooner.' So there it was: they'd withheld hospital treatment. 'My dad did it,' the girl said, staring at Marie.

Marie considered this. She knew men were brutes. Big Ted's fur was grey and matted. Like he'd spent some time at the bottom of Nelson Creek.

'I'll need to reattach his arm and eye, re-stuff and stitch him up. Give his fur a good clean. I could have him ready by next Tuesday.'

The mother said that would be fine.

'But Mum,' Ava interrupted, 'we're gonna visit Aunt Cath.'

'Sweetheart, we'll come back to get Big Ted.'

Marie watched them cross the road and go inside Janey's Coffee Shoppe. She'd been sitting here, at her work table, ever since. With bobbles, birch needles, glass eyes. First, she pulled out Ted's wet, grey stuffing. Used baby wipes to clean his fur. Got the hair-dryer out.

Re-stuffed him with white cotton clouds. Sewed the seams up. And smiled.

She'd grown up during the war, knew the value of hard work. As a child, she had one teddy bear, a treasured gift, and she made him t-shirts and hats out of her mother's fabric scraps. Buttercup slept in a shoebox-bed beside her own. Came to school with her. One of the worst things that ever happened in Marie's life – and there were lots of terrible things – was losing him on the inner-suburban train line.

There. She'd succeeded in reattaching the arm. She chose a thick gauze bandage from the drawer, and wound it around Big Ted's arm, clipping it with a pin. 'Good as new,' she said. 'Almost.' She carried him carefully to the shelves where the patients rested in alphabetical order. Big Ted went next to Big Ears and Biggy. The rest of the patients – plush bears, rabbits, wombats, elephants, along with one tiger, seal and two kangaroos – were sleeping peacefully. She tucked in Big Ted and kissed his cheek.

Although Marie had started with teddy bears – she was still learning the trade then – she'd expanded her business in recent years, taking in all plush animals. Crocodiles. Dolphins. Koalas. Whatever came her way. She'd even hired an assistant, a young man with a long face but cheerful manner. It was nice to have someone else around. The shop got too quiet, especially at night, when the customers, the girls and boys and their parents, were sound asleep in their goose-down beds, on the other side of town.

The clock told her it was ten past eight, but she couldn't go home. Still had a few patients to attend to. When she'd first moved to this town thirty years ago, she hadn't known how violent kids could be with their toys. They brought her decapitated bears, kangaroos without tails, and tigers sawn in half. Often they blamed siblings or friends, but Marie knew better. Believed in personal responsibility.

The town's population was 3,500. About a quarter were young kids. And half of those, at some point in their young lives, would bring their beloved toys to Marie for mending.

'Big Ted, you poor bear. What happened?'

He kept his face turned away.

'Ava's dad threw you in the creek, didn't he? Some men are no good. I would know, too. Isn't that—'

'Marie?'

She spun around.

'Yes, Aidan?'

She was comfortable around him; he didn't mind her talking to the animals.

'I'm heading out for the night, unless there's something you need?'

'No, no. Go home.' She smiled. 'I'll see you tomorrow. We can talk about Polly the Panda Bear in the morning.'

She watched Aidan shuffle up the hill to his parents' place.

He'd only been here for about six months but he was a quick learner. When he'd first applied for the job, she'd asked him, 'But why are you interested in working in a bear hospital?' and he'd said, 'Why not?' and so that was that. He was actually great with customers, especially the parents. Never blamed them for the horrible injuries.

Marie got the ledger down to fill with the day's orders. The final entry was for poor old Big Ted.

Customer's name: Ava Smith (Mother: Jessica Smith)

Patient's Name: Big Ted

Ailment: Wet stuffing. Missing foot, left. Missing glass eye, right. Matted fur.

Treatment: Reattachment of foot and eye. Re-stuffing. Carpet cleaner on fur, brush with wire bristles.

Cost: $12

Collection date: 8/12

She knew she'd undercharged. Something about the girl's stony eyes had startled her. The girl knew what a bad place the world could be. Marie recognised herself in those eyes. Not that she believed in self-examination – self-excavation, more like. Earth-moving equipment churning up her insides.

She wished Big Ted a goodnight and turned off the lights. As always, she kept the owl night light on. Couldn't bear the thought of all those animals alone in the dark.

Pulling down the roller door, she glanced up and down the street, then walked the six blocks to her house, under those awful plane trees, craving a nice strong whisky.

*

She was examining Big Ted when a customer rang the bell. The woman was wearing a red skirt, her hair still damp from the morning rain.

'Hello?' she said, pushing a plush crocodile, half-chewed, across the counter. 'Can you believe our pet Collie did that?'

Marie hated dogs. They were too jumpy. Unpredictable. Like all living animals. She took Mr Snap into her arms, and rotated him from side to side.

'All he needs is some extra stuffing, bit of re-stitching. And he'll be good as new.'

The woman was pleased with that.

After the customer left, Marie picked up Big Ted. 'I think I'll do the glass eye next,' she told Aidan.

He was ordering sewing supplies for the store, cotton stuffing, tea and coffee. They drank Earl Grey at all times of day.

'Loose leaf or tea bags?' he asked.

'Both, please. Tea bags are good for when you're in a hurry.'

They had a lot of work this time of year. Mending was cheaper than buying new.

She tried to match Big Ted's remaining amber eye. She held a few glass eyes up to the empty socket until she found the right shape and colour.

She doubled a golden thread that matched the bear's fur, then doubled it again so that it was slightly longer than the width of his head. Then she threaded the glass eye. The next bit was barbaric.

'I'll be gentle,' she said to Big Ted.

'Does the patient need anaesthetic?' Aidan joked, kindly.

She smiled at him. He was too young to understand. How the fate of toys said a lot about their owners.

She picked up a doll needle and carefully threaded it. She then aimed it at the exact spot where she wanted the eye to go. Pushing the needle through Big Ted's head to the base of his soft skull, the glass eye sat nicely in the socket.

She exhaled. Secured the threads and returned Big Ted to his shelf. 'There,' she said. She hated to think what would've happened if Big Ted hadn't come to the hospital.

'The tip,' Aidan said. 'That's where they all end up.'

She didn't go in for funerals or memorials even though Aidan thought it'd make them money. 'For the terminal cases,' he'd said.

Marie worked on Big Ted over the next few days, while other jobs filled the ledger. Tensions ran high in households in December. Everyone was just bloody tired, of work and each other. Parents dropped off mangled and battered bears and rabbits. Occasionally, you'd see a botched home operation.

Marie delegated to Aidan where she could.

'For the farm animals, use a little carpet cleaner,' she said. 'Small circular motions.'

'The squeaky mechanism inside the chicken is faulty. See if you can find a replacement with a similar squeak.'

'Gary needs to have his left ossicone reattached.'

Aidan frowned. 'Ossicone?'

'The outcropping of bone between a giraffe's ears.'

'Got it.'

'See what you can make of Polly the Panda Bear. The mother says her daughter is convinced he isn't the same. That something's wrong.'

'Sounds like Munchausen by proxy to me.'

'Might be. But we want to investigate before suggesting the daughter see a shrink.'

The two of them worked side by side, Aidan occasionally bringing in cups of Early Grey, which is what they started calling *Earl Grey*, because they had their first cuppa at seven. Classic FM was on the radio, and the windows closed to the plane trees. Marie had sensitive lungs.

She worked the wire bristle brush – normally used for brushing a dog's fur – back and forth across Big Ted until his fur became fluffy again. When she finished, he looked brand new. Less scruffy, but still recognisably Big Ted.

'He's beautiful,' Aidan said.

She agreed.

She put him back on the shelf under 'B' and marked him ready for collection. She waited for Ava and her mother to return.

Tuesday then Wednesday came around, but Ava and her mother didn't come to collect Big Ted. They didn't stop by the next or the next day. Marie started to worry that something might have happened. She picked up the receiver and dialled their home. A gruff male voice picked up.

'Hello?' it said.

'Hi, my name is Marie and I'm calling from the Bear Hospital. Is this the Smith residence?'

'It is.'

'Is Jessica there? Her daughter's plush toy is ready for pick up.'

'Not stupid Big Ted?'

Marie was appalled.

'Look, they're not actually here. But I can come and collect the bear.'

Marie paused. 'You know,' she said, 'I might just hold on to him.'

'Why don't I just stop by and get him? I need to get back in Ava's good books if you know what I mean.' He laughed a smoker's laugh.

'Only the person named on the ledger can pick it up—' that was a complete lie '—but if you could please let Jessica know I called, I'd really appreciate it.'

The man said that he would and hung up.

Cradling Big Ted in her arms, she told Aidan that he was theirs now, at least for the time being. 'He can watch over the store until Ava returns.'

Another week passed and Marie felt more and more uneasy. Only a handful of plush animals were never collected. It was usually a bad sign. Of ill-health or injury.

Where did the mother say they were going? To visit an aunt? She knew from personal experience that when home life was rocky, kids needed their soft toys more than ever.

If someone had returned Buttercup, Marie thought her life could've been different. She might never have worked at the Bear Hospital, but also perhaps her mother would've stayed. Buttercup was both best friend and protective charm.

What was the aunt's name? Something commonplace. Karen? Kathy? Cath. It was Cath, short for Catherine then.

'They probably don't want to be found,' Aidan said.

That was probably true – they didn't want to be found by the dad – but Marie knew that Ava needed Big Ted no matter what.

Assuming that Catherine was Jessica's sister, they needed to find out Jessica's maiden name. The town's Presbyterian Church yielded nothing, but the Anglican Church held the marriage record they were looking for.

Aidan got down the White Pages from behind the counter and together they looked up Catherine Reilly.

'Sixteen of them!'

They started from the top, and rang four Catherine Reillys before a pause on the line told her they'd found the right one.

'Who did you say you were?' Cath asked.

When Jessica came on the line, she sounded wary.

'How on earth did you find us?'

'*The White Pages*,' Marie said. 'I was worried when you didn't come back to the shop.'

Jessica was silent.

'You must think it strange for me to call you out of the blue. I'm sentimental when it comes to toys—' she was actually very practical '—and I thought Ava might want Big Ted back. Why don't I go ahead and mail him to you?'

Later that afternoon Marie walked to the post office with a bear-shaped parcel.

The customers gossiped about Harry Smith. No-one had seen Jessica or Ava in weeks.

'A loose cannon,' said a customer collecting a once mangy wombat.

'Raving at the neighbours,' someone else told Aidan.

'I heard he keeps a Samurai sword by the door.'

One evening walking home, Marie thought she saw Ava in a passing car. But no, it was another little girl with ribboned hair.

A week earlier, Marie had leapt over a crate of spare parts to pick up the ringing phone.

'Has my wife collected Big Ted?'

It was Harry Smith.

Marie lied. 'No.'

'So they're still out woop woop.'

'Sorry?'

'Bloody Cath,' he said before hanging up.

For days, Marie worried she'd said the wrong thing.

The plane trees inflamed her lungs as the gossip continued. She had more and more coughing fits. Aidan was attentive, bringing in cups of *Early Grey* and Melba toast. He shushed customers when they talked about Harry Smith.

A few weeks later a bear-shaped package arrived at the shop with the words 'Return to Sender' in black texta. On the front, a series of forwarding addresses, each crossed out.

Marie coughed and coughed and coughed.

It looked like Ava and Jessica had been on the move. And if the post couldn't find them, Marie hoped that meant Harry couldn't either.

Big Ted sat beside the till, keeping watch over the store. Amber eyes shining. Marie sewed him hats and vests. Ties and pants. The bear had a knack for comforting kids. Out of all the toys in the store, they were drawn to him.

When Marie died some twenty years later, Aidan took over the Bear Hospital. In her lifetime, she'd never seen Ava or her mother in town again, but had always hoped they'd come back, and maybe someday they would.

Big Ted was ready.

Acknowledgments

I would like to thank Spineless Wonders' publisher Bronwyn Mehan and editor Kalhari Jayaweera for their generous support and valuable assistance in bringing this collection to publication.

The Writing NSW Varuna Fellowship 2019 gave me the time and space to think and to write. A big thank you to Fiona Maplestone who kindly gave me permission to tell the story in 'Picket Fence'.

Thank you to Helen Meany, Ruth Armstrong, Suzanne Boccalatte, Liz Tasker, Brigitte Trenear, David Naylor, Harry Goddard, Sarah Bellingham, Pip Smith, Sam Twyford-Moore and Fiona Wright for reading and editing many of the stories in *Grub*.

Thank you to Ida Lawrence and the extended Ridge Street family for keeping me safe, amused and inspired over the years.

Thanks Mum and Dad and Nan and Alex for slipping me some money here and there, and for reading my stuff.

Previous Publications

Three stories in this collection have been previously published as follows:

'*Honey and the landlord in the attic*', Visible Ink, 2017

'*Whipped Cream*', UTS Anthology 2018

'*Artichoke Hearts*', Mascara Literary Review 2018.

Biography

Tanya Vavilova is a queer writer preoccupied with liminal spaces and outsider perspectives—by life on the margins. She has published work in *Meanjin*, *Mascara Literary Review*, *Westerly*, *Seizure*, *The Lifted Brow*, and *UTS Writers' Anthology*. Her writing has won the Copyright Agency's Cultural Fund Best Prose and Wollongong Writers Festival Short Story Prize, and has been commended or shortlisted for the Newcastle Short Story Award, Overland's Fair Australia and Neilma Sidney prizes, and the Seizure Viva La Novella, among others. Her debut collection of essays, *We are Speaking in Code*, was released in 2020. Grub is her debut collection of short stories and won the Carmel Bird Digital Literary Award in 2019.

About This Series

Grub by Tanya Vavilova is published as part of the Spineless Wonders Smalls series of small format paperbacks released to celebrate our tenth year in publishing.

To find out about other books published in this series, go to www.shortaustralianstories.com.au